A NOTE ON THE AUTHOR

Lucy Brydon is a writer and filmmaker from Edinburgh. A graduate of Warwick University with a First Class BA (Hons) in English Literature and Creative Writing, Lucy moved to Shanghai in 2005 and lived there for four and half years.

During that time, Lucy worked briefly as a token Western hostess in a nightclub to pay her rent. The bizarre but heady life of a barfly proved to be the inspiration for her first novel, *Shanghai Passenger*.

Lucy is currently based in London.

Shanghai Passenger

LUCY BRYDON

BLUE MARK BOOKS

1

First published in Great Britain by
Blue Mark Books Limited in 2015

www.bluemarkbooks.com

© Lucy Brydon 2015

Jacket artwork © Heather Morgan

A catalogue record for this book is
available from the British Library

ISBN 978-1-910369-09-8

Blue Mark Books Limited supports the Forest Stewardship Council®. The
FSC® promotes the responsible management of the world's forests.
All our books carrying the FSC® logo are printed on FSC®-certified paper

MIX
Paper from
responsible sources
FSC® C013604

Typeset in Adobe Caslon Pro by
Blue Mark Books Limited

Printed and bound by
CPI Group (UK) Ltd, CR0 4YY

"Once upon a time, I dreamt I was a butterfly, fluttering hither and thither, to all intents and purposes a butterfly. I was conscious only of my happiness as a butterfly, unaware that I was myself. Soon I awaked, and there I was, veritably myself again. Now I do not know whether I was then a man dreaming I was a butterfly, or whether I am now a butterfly, dreaming I am a man."

– Zhuangzi.

One

Shanghai. Nanjing Road. A glass smashing into a glass. Senseless as your dreams. The Paris of the East, the whore of the Orient. A fluorescent version of the future complete with unique selling points. Everything about this long road makes you want to move faster. To keep up with an imagined race. A twenty-three year-old, unemployed wannabe; the antibody or the foreign body? I can't tell. I should have anticipated this.

Street signs dissolve into nothing. Behind and ahead, the flow of human heads merges into a mass of black hair and thick jackets. "MissMissYouSoBeautiful," a seller calls, holding a card with pictures of handbags on it in my direction. Is he talking to me? I wave him away. He shouts to another wag. They both laugh.

Is this it?

Young men and women shout, faceless in the crowd. Mantras from all angles.

"MissMissMissYouWannaBuyShoesYouWannaBuyBag?"

This must be the new wave *hello*.

It's colder than I expected. I never check the forecasts. I assumed it would be sunny because I wanted it to be. What did I pack? Summer dresses, I think.

What I remember of the night I left London: vodka, highs, notebooks, goodbyes. The necessities. Goodbye to all that, then. Can I leave it behind?

Playing the star in the movie adaptation of my life, I can. These moments, when you believe you can do anything. So foolish yet so precious.

A dragon of strip lights and fire streams its plastic flames out of a window that lies ahead. Perhaps this is sanctuary? I stop.

A seller in front of me gestures dismissively to the bundles of woollens on display at her stand and reaches under it for a box. She holds out a thin scarf decorated with fishes.

"Silk, silk," the woman says, another monotone mantra. "Good price for you."

I opt for a black cardigan at the back of the row of bundles and ignore the scarf. Disheartened, she tosses it back in the box and puts the cardigan in a bag. Handing it over, she shows me a piece of jade with ancient script carved into it.

"This good luck," she tells me, her sentences broken but the essentials all intact. "This Tang Dynasty poetry. And made from jade! Fifty year old!"

There are chips all over it. But chipped luck is better than no luck, I suppose. Maybe luck is a commodity, too.

"DiorPradaGucciFendiBagWatchShoe," a girl calls from the opposite stall. I wander away from the group, the most conspicuous I have ever been. The foreign devil.

"No Gucci right now," I call back.

The girl runs after me. She tugs on my arm, rough and desperate. "Come!" she shouts. A stir of charity or curiosity. I follow her.

Off Nanjing Road, the gutters are littered with empty cans, bottles, nappies, used chopsticks and Styrofoam containers. A young man approaches the rusty bikes that are dotting our path. Kneeling down, he starts to strip the leather from the seats with a Stanley knife.

The girl opens a door. To the left, another door is wedged ajar into a room lined with full bookcases. In the centre, a child lies on a dirty beanbag playing a game on a mobile phone.

"*Ni tai tiaopi!*" she chastises the boy in Mandarin. As he runs away with the phone, she turns to me with a world-weary expression crumpling her forehead. "My son is naughty boy!"

Pulling a bookcase aside, she reveals a shelving unit with a library of DVDs and a selection of knock off watches, shoes and handbags. I shake my head. She slides the bookcase back, muttering under her breath.

Outside, the boy at the bikes is now attacking the rubber on the wheels. The muscles on his back contort in rhythm with his hands. As I thank the girl and walk away, she yells out again, giving the sale one last shot.

"*Wo gei ni hen pian yi! Zhen de!*" And then in English, "I give you big discount!"

At the corner, another girl holds her shitting baby over the stoop of a house. Onto the frenzied anonymity of Nanjing Dong Road, I forget everything but the Pearl Tower, settling back into the distance and absent from boys stripping bikes and DiorPradaGucciFendiBag-WatchShoe. An everyman's spaceship overlooking the inhabitants of its city with a knowing eye, it manages to simultaneously wink at the nocturnal happenings and myself. At a forgotten past and a lascivious future. I feel that sense of intimacy one experiences with great landmarks.

This is it.

*

Pirates, the hostel I picked at random, has metal studs on the steps and floors. The walls are hung with lifebelts. On the menu board, *Walk The Plank Stew* and *Cutlass Potato Wedges* are offered as specials. The girl at reception has the number 40403 instead of a name on her badge, but introduces herself as Mindy. I pay Mindy and tell her I'll think about whether or not I want to extend the five-night stay. It could be longer. Who knows? I don't.

As Mindy leads the way up the stairs towards my room, talk and cooking smells filter down from the rooftop bar. Dreadlocked travellers chat on the landing, their conversation about Thailand conducted in estuary English accents.

Room 404 smells like cleaning fluid mixed with green tea. No mess, no fuss. Nothing like that. Mindy thanks me and closes the door behind her.

Peace, relief. From chaos, make order. Not spontaneous this time. Order has never been my strong point. Oh well. The last song I heard comes into my head. What was it? *Ruby Tuesday* by the Rolling

Stones.

I put the dresses away in the wardrobe. The scrappy notebook and the new Moleskine are positioned firmly on the desk. It's a bit self-important to be buying Moleskines. Fuck it. This is an odyssey. It deserves a new notebook. Journey to the east, and all that. I like this process of distillation. I like it very much.

A pot-pourried bathroom. A mirror. My reflected face. Overall, slightly above average on a good day. Self-hating narcissism is a bitch to handle.

I take off my clothes and locate the white towel and the wrapped up soaps and miniature shampoo bottles that smell of ocean. The water from the shower spills over my body, seeping through the cracks in tiles. This is where I have wanted to be for a very long time. You never know it until you're there. Escape is the guaranteed route to renewal. Washing your body only does so much. Washing your life is far more effective.

Drying off, I glance out the window onto the lanes below. A female voice is calling out in low intonations. To a lover? Damn these romantic assumptions.

I lie back on the bed. Almost instantly there is black.

*

Feeling the branch beneath her feet, the caterpillar's first thought was of relief at being born. Relief turned to wonder as the caterpillar began to examine all that was in her world. Wonder at the roughness of the bark beneath her. Wonder at the oily surfaces of the leaves around her. Wonder at the blue sky, the green grass, the brown dirt beneath that grass.

"This is how it starts," the caterpillar thought, looking back at the fleshy jewel from which she had just emerged.

Two

I wake up and check the clock I adjusted when I got off the plane. Eleven pm. Time to go out into the wild. I walk to the desk that makes a stab at being a kitchenette, basking in the novelty of naked coffee making.

Turning on the shower, I find that most of the fake ocean shower soap has gone. I dab the remainder in the necessary areas. As I put my makeup on, my hair dries over my face in a too long curl. Oh well.

I put on three summer dresses, one on top of the other. It doesn't look quite as bad as I would have guessed. The cardigan is, upon closer examination, not attractive at all – the sleeves have puffy shoulders and the buttons are fake crystal something-or-other – but temperatures dictate that I wear it. Damn these impulse purchases.

The noises wafting from the top floor lead me upstairs to the bar, *Captain*. Half a boat hangs from the wall. The curved ceilings collect smoke from the few punters who are in situ. First plus point for China. Fuck health and safety. You've got to love a country that appreciates that a glass of wine and a cigarette is one of the greatest small pleasures going.

I order a gin and tonic. A dude in his sixties approaches from the left and gives me a becoming stare. He has silver-rimmed, tinted glasses. Beads of sweat collect on his brow. It is the face of a man who is on the run for a crime he definitely committed.

Turning away from Kiddy Fiddler, I notice a blonde girl and a Chinese man on a squashy sofa. A faux coat of arms, engraved with the words 'Just Undo It', swings over their heads.

The girl catches my eye and waves; proof that comfort in strangers is possible. There is an open bottle of champagne on the table and they certainly don't look earnest enough to be planning a whistle-stop

5

museum tour for tomorrow. I make my way over.

Close-up, the girl must be in her mid-twenties. The structure of her face is a photographer's dream; all high cheekbones and full lips. As I sink into the sofa next to her, she introduces herself as Rose.

"I'm from Melbourne," she says, handing me a glass of champagne.

"You don't have the accent."

"I left when I was fourteen."

"What have you been doing with yourself?" I ask.

"Trying to avoid other commitments in any way, shape or form wherever possible. I just arrived here yesterday. What's your name?"

"Ruby Tuesday," I reply, wondering if she'll get the joke. I might never see her again, after all.

"You can tell me what you're really called another time." Yes, she is my sort of buddy. "Harold finished his thesis on Chinese opera today," she says of her companion, "so we're celebrating."

"Congratulations." I lift my champagne towards Harold. "I just arrived here so you'll have to show me around."

"Welcome to Shanghai," Harold replies, his face flushed with the alcohol. "I've never met a redhead before."

"Don't you love celebrations?" Rose clinks our glasses with hers. "Whatever they might be for?"

I get the sense that she might be the sort of person who is quick at making friends. She talks with the scattergun conversational approach of one who knows how to entertain.

"It must be fun to be an actress," Harold says.

"I can't do anything else," she replies.

Not being able to do anything else. It's how I feel about writing. When I'm actually doing it, that is. As opposed to procrastinating about doing it while doing other things.

"Selfie!" Rose says, holding out her Smartphone. Harold leans in. Rose grabs my arm.

"I don't selfie," I say.

"Are you a Taoist?" Rose says, pulling Harold close.

"I don't think they say anything about selfies in Taoism."

After a few rounds of adjustment, Rose takes a picture that she is prepared to share on social media. Spent, Harold flops back in his chair as Rose examines the images on her phone.

"And what do you do?" Harold asks me.

It would be so easy to lie and make out like I'm some sort of big shot. I bet expatriates do it all the time. I opt for the more complicated truth.

"Shop assistant. Lifeguard attendant. Customer sales advisor. The list goes on. I got fired from every job I've ever had. I spent most of my last pay on the plane ticket over here. I want to write a book but I procrastinate a lot and have a tendency to get distracted by having a good time."

The book to end all books. The book to bestow my genius gifts unto an unknowing and uncaring world. Or alternatively, a rambling estimate of life as an urban nomad. Probably the latter.

"I like your honesty," Rose says, putting the phone into her handbag.

The waiter comes to take a plate of leftover crab away and we order another bottle. *Just one more, just one more:* the refrain that has so often landed me in bother. I make a mental note that tomorrow I will almost definitely start the book.

"Shanghai's hard to leave," Harold says. "It's the right place for a good time. I've seen people go and come back so many times. There's nowhere quite like it."

"We've only just got here!" Rose says.

When the champagne arrives I make another mental note that even if I'm not working on the book, the book must – in a small capacity, surely – be working on me. So, by that equation, either way I am working. I like this logic very much. It is also known as wishful thinking.

*

In the bathroom I'm struck by the intricacies of the Chinese graffiti on the walls. It probably says 'I WOZ ERE', or one of those other toilet stall philosophies written when you are fucked up at four in the morning. Surely in China they must have the international language of drunken girls scrawling what they suppose to be universal truths?

Although not drunk, I'm in the mood to leave my mark and take a pen from my bag. *In Vino Veritas*, I write. As an afterthought I add the translation. I pull my knickers up and flush the toilet.

Outside, Harold and Rose are waiting. The nautical steps have taken on an Escher quality after all the booze. 40403's eyes follow us as we make our way out into the night.

The wind belts us and I feel the effect – or lack – of my preposterous outfit. I must go shopping tomorrow on top of writing my novel. No one will ever realise how much I have to do tomorrow. Every single tomorrow.

Is this laziness? Sloth is the least antagonistic sin, I suppose.

Past the art deco hotels on Fuzhou Road, we reach People's Square and the park as the lights on several of the taller skyscrapers are switched off. Shanghai, a second ago so spectacular, is suddenly the girl who arrives at a party wearing a fur coat and then takes it off to reveal a plain black dress underneath. But I've always liked cities best when they are denuded. Anything is pretty in the right light.

Harold leads us through a rabbit warren of low-rises. Middle-aged couples play *mahjong* on the street corner, sipping from tea canisters. Two young men harness at least forty Styrofoam boxes onto the back of a bicycle; one is on the ground and the other stands wobbling on the cross bar. After a few attempts, they push off with their bounty.

Inside one of the flats, seven people cluster around a tiny box that is blaring out pop music. They all have their shirts off, laughing at whatever is being shown on the screen. We follow the route out of the slums. On the other side is a fifteen-story shopping centre with real DiorPradaGucciFendiBagWatchShoe.

Squalor one side, skyscrapers on the other. This is it.

*

Shortly after we arrive at *Wallflower*, a gay bar hidden through narrow passages I will not remember in daytime, Harold says he has to leave for Suzhou but that he will be back in town soon and he would love to meet us again. Rose gives him her number. Harold kisses us each on both cheeks four times and tells us to have a wonderful time. Then he's gone.

"I always wanted to be an actress," Rose says for the second time, drinking up the last of Harold's gin and eyeing the clientele. There's house music on; a beat produced by a machine scientifically designed to get people to dance. A punk and a mod are canoodling, hands straying. I've never met a working actress before, but it strikes me that they talk about acting as much as writers talk about writing.

"We're all actors," she says. "We're all pretending. All the time. So it's at least an authentic way to make a living. A license to be whoever you want. My main thing is theatre, the immediacy."

I appreciate this purism.

Despite the fact that we are now residing in China, I realise that neither of us knows much about the country itself.

"Ting and Ming, Ping and Pong," Rose says, when I ask if she's tried to learn the lingo.

The punk and the mod foxtrot in a dark corner, whispering in each others' ear. Sweat descends and their faces start to merge into one.

"Shall we move on?" I ask.

Leaving *Wallflower*, we walk back past the park in the direction we came in. Dominoes now, the buildings cast watchful eyes over us. Figures move behind curtains. New people, same actions. Eating, screwing, cleaning up their own mess. What people do.

As we turn another corner and head towards the Bund, Rose says that she's going to search for a flat tomorrow.

"What are your plans?" she asks.

"I don't know." Yes I do.

"We could get a place together. We're both here for a good time."

That's too easy. Besides, I have other things to do tomorrow. Shopping for clothes and writing a novel. Nobody realises how much I have to do tomorrow.

"Oh, all right," I reply. I hate myself.

9

Bar Bleu is the sort of place that becomes pleasurable only after damage has been done in the recreational drug department. Rose shows me the baggie in her hand. Evidently she's a friend of Colombia, too. We make off to the toilets for a line.

Propped up, Rose quickly befriends one of the many French businessmen in attendance, Alexandre. I am left with his friend. It quickly becomes clear that we have nothing in common apart from the fact that we are both Caucasians in Asia. Pierre – at least, I think it's Pierre – talks enough for both of us, regardless of my stuttering utterances.

"So, *donc*, when I'm selling ad space for the beeeeg companeez…"

I'm so high, all I keep catching is the phrase beeeeg companeez. I repeat it over and over in my head. After half an hour it seems rude to ask his name again. It also stands to reason that if he's an average sort of French man he could in all likelihood be called Pierre. Pierre it is.

I tune out and put on the internal radio. Something uptempo.

La la la.

*

Much later, when the four of us reach yet another set of crossroads by the dockside, my ability to process the passage of time in an accurate way has signed off for the evening. Is it six or seven am?

"It's over there!" Alexandre says. I would be less cynical if it weren't the fifteenth time he'd said this, but follow the others to a dock where a row of yachts is moored.

"So, do you 'ave a kilt?" Pierre says, his eyes moving down my legs. I wish I hadn't told him I'm from Scotland. He's been banging on about the 'natural affeeeenity' between the Scots and the French since we started walking.

"This is it!" Alexandre says, disrupting my inner quandary about whether or not to answer Pierre's question. He waves at a uniformed man who lowers the access ladder to an enormous boat with *Bad Karma* emblazoned on the side.

Rose jumps the white railings and holds out her hand, pulling me over. When I put my foot down on the other side, my ankle goes over itself. I almost topple into the river but Alexandre steadies me.

The engine breaks into a burr as Alexandre shows us around. Three floors, a terrace. Of course, this immaculate staging was to be expected. I nearly fall over again on the wrought iron staircase to the cabin. Well, if I died on the steps of a yacht in high heels it would be more glamorous than a nursing home in a few decades time. And I'd still look decent in a coffin.

The living area has a walnut brown interior, stereo, circular daybed and white leather sofas. Rose helps herself to the champagne chilling in a cooler. Alexandre leads a toast.

"We should welcome the ladies, *non*?" Pierre's smile is not far away from lecherous. Alexandre ignores Pierre and nestles next to Rose.

"To good living!" Alexandre says, raising his glass.

The roar of the motor booms louder as the boat shifts away from the dock. Puxi slowly diminishes from view. Alexandre turns to me.

"Where are you staying, the same place as Rose?"

"Yes, *Pirates*."

"*Pirates*? What is this *Pirates*?" He says, confused.

"The Hyatt," Rose rolls her eyes at me from behind Alexandre's back.

"Oh!" Alexandre laughs at himself. "It must be my English."

Alexandre picks up on a lecture about Chinese language he had begun earlier in the evening but abandoned when Rose leant over him in her low-cut top.

"The simplicity. It's why I fall in love with it." He waves his hand to the opposite side of the river.

"*Par exemple*, Pudong. River East. No tenses, either. I teach you some expressions. The first is *ni hao*, hello. The second is *xie xie*, thank you. And the third…"

"Why must there be any more?" Pierre interrupts. "There's no need to learn. This all you really need."

"The good things always come in three. You're only 'ere for the dollars and the pussy, anyway," Alexandre teases Pierre, whose eyes flitter moodily towards Pudong.

Alexandre cuts a line, snorts, and offers me the rolled up note. I do the line. It's a strong hit. I am wilder, sharper and more interesting than seconds ago.

"So, girls, I tell you the third important expression here in China," Alexandre says. "TIC. Stands for This Is China. It explain all the things that make no sense. You an outsider. You a *laowai*. You in a different psychological landscape, now. Things happen and there is no logical explanation for them."

Rose tucks her legs underneath her, pointing them towards Alexandre's pelvis. He puts his arm around her shoulder. This might be a good time to head upstairs for a smoke.

The river traces frothy undulations on the bow. In the distance, Puxi is the mistress left behind. The captain's silhouette falls onto the terrace from the crew room. In his fifties, he is kitted out in full sailor garb, complete with hat.

"Hello, Miss!" he calls. "Welcome aboard!"

Footsteps move from the stern in my direction, breaking the slap of lapping water.

"Ah, you are hiding from me?" comes Pierre's voice, in a tone I assume he intends to be playful but only serves to underscore my opinion of him.

Opinion of Pierre: tosser.

"Yes."

For a second he is unsure whether or not to laugh. He does.

"You're funny," he says.

"Did you ever play that game when you were a kid? Port and starboard?" I ask him.

"*Non*. What is it?"

I'm about to try and explain it to him when I realise that I don't remember the rules. Another conversational black hole. Yes, silence is golden.

He smokes two drags of his cigarette and flicks it into the river.

12

"It's chilly!" he says, turning on his heel and heading back to the cabin. I look down into the choppy depths. Either it's to get away from Pierre or just for the hell of it, but for a second I want to jump.

The little voyage comes to an end and the boat slides back into its mooring. The one sign of life in Puxi is a group of workers whose building site is pitched a few hundred metres from *Bad Karma's* spot. They position and reposition a tube of scaffold that is at least the length of a football pitch, creating what is destined to be the newest fixture on the skyline.

A gust of wind picks up, probing at the tube. For a moment, it looks like they might drop it. The shortest worker darts underneath to steady it. In a peculiar ballet, they manage to place it in the correct position.

As the hum of the boat's engine fades to nothing, Pierre puts a warm hand on my hip.

"We should leave them," he says.

"Is she okay?" I move away from the hand, wondering whether or not to wait.

"She will get what she is asking for."

Escape being the only option, I climb over the railing. Pierre tries to help steady me. Preferring to take my chances with a watery end, I jump.

I pick up the pace on the pavement as Pierre hotfoots it after me. A taxi snakes towards us, its light a gleaming invitation. There are several strategies here. The first being that I simply get in the taxi and don't invite him to join. The second being I let him take the taxi. There is a third but I don't really want to think about it.

"So… how do you like your eggs in ze morning?" Pierre says.

"Unfertilised," I reply, stopping. It's true.

A pause. "I don't understand."

"I'm politely telling you to fuck off. But I was using humour, hoping that you would get the message. However, it doesn't seem to be working. So to be clear – I definitely, one hundred percent do not want to have any kind of penetrative intercourse with you. At all."

"I was trying to be friendly. Can I have your phone number?"

13

"I don't have a phone." This is also true.

"What?"

The workmen, now on a fag break, watch the scene.

"I don't have a phone."

"How do you… survive?"

"I'm here, aren't I?"

Crossing the road, I catch the eye of the tallest workman. Still drunk, I make a sweeping courtesy to the group, who start to clap as Pierre retreats to *Bad Karma*. *Je ne regrette* fucking *rien*.

Drops flit from the sky, bringing the old ego back to reality.

Where to now?

*

The caterpillar looked up to the top of the tree. As she moved further along the branch, more colours and textures emerged from the same fragments of her sphere. The caterpillar was glad to see them all before her. They were more interesting than the insides of the fleshy jewel.

"I must not lose the ability to wonder," the caterpillar thought. "If I lose that, I might as well not be here at all."

Three

Rose and I meet for a late breakfast in the hostel café. Ingesting coffee and mentholated cigarettes, I adjust to the stark reality of being awake again. It's a bit early for communication of the verbal sort. Mornings aren't my thing. In fact, morning people, or people who describe themselves as morning people, are generally to be bracketed in the 'peppy' category. Peppy types deserve ridicule as a general rule. But then, if I ruled the world most of it would be conducted naked in bed, accompanied by red wine, and nothing would ever get done.

Rose has already researched flats online and made an appointment to see a studio. I take in this startling efficiency as I stir my coffee. I am very much in the thrall of such efficiency.

"It's got two bedrooms and it's cheap as chips," she says, excitedly.

Rose is amused by the details of the previous evening's attempted seduction. Overhearing the story, a nearby waiter bites his bottom lip in an effort not to smirk. Picking up Rose's empty cup, he makes his way past the table on the other side of us which is commandeered by boys in their late teens. All of them are staring at smartphones instead of talking to each other.

"What happened with Alexandre?"

"Bit of a kiss, no bury the sausage. I realised I hadn't shaved my legs so I gave him my number instead. We'll see."

"I'm sure he'll respect you more in the long run," I say, dryly.

"Respect, bullshit. I told you, I'm a commitment-phobe anyway. That's what bisexuals are. We're enigmas. Sometimes with men, sometimes with women. Unpredictable creatures."

"You're bi?"

"Well, I'd say more 'quadsexual'. As in – I can take it from girls but I can't give it. Do you know what I mean?"

"Selfish-sexual?" At least she has the grace to laugh.

"I had one bone fide *girl* girlfriend. It was a couple of years ago. Her name was Luella and she was from…" she strains for the memory, "Norway. I was listening to a lot of dyke rock at the time and she looked a bit like a dude so I thought I could give it a go. She kept giving me head. But when push came to shove, so to speak, I couldn't touch her bits. I got away with six times of pretending to fall asleep right afterwards but then she got suspicious. I told her that I wasn't gay enough to give her head back," Rose warms to her story, "I don't fancy clam chowder. She then took offence and told me that I wasn't gay at all. Then I got offended because I'm definitely a *bit* gay and sexuality is a spectrum anyway. We both started to cry and I left. I guess that's why I shouldn't go out with chicks, although I do fancy women occasionally. There's too much sensitivity involved. And then the cycles line up and it's just a menstrual storm in a teacup."

I laugh so hard that coffee comes out of my nose.

"I think you just set the feminist movement back about sixty years," I tell her, rubbing the coffee dribble from my face with a tissue.

"I *am* a feminist," she says, all sincerity. More coffee dribble.

Twenty-first century feminist: female chauvinist lipstick lesbian. Apparently.

*

While Nanjing Dong Road is less of a hustle when we step out, the energy is still deep and still on. We each buy a pancake filled with eggs, chives and chilli fresh from an elderly lady's stall.

A taxi driver slows and winds down his window. Rose shows him the address in pinyin on her phone. The taxi driver takes it and lifts his spectacles onto his forehead. He attempts to read it then hands the phone back, shaking his head.

"Chong Ching," I say, feeling like a racist from an eighties sitcom. "Chong Ching?" The driver is mystified.

"Chong Ching," Rose says.

"Chong Ching?" The driver is none the wiser.

"Chong Ching!" I try to make it sound like I know what I'm talking about.

"Ahhhhh!" He turns the key in the ignition. "*Chongqing Nan Lu!*"

"Ok?" I ask. Surely he must understand that?

"Ok!"

"I thought the agent was taking the piss over the phone," Rose mutters as we pile into the back seat, possibly on the right route to the unknown destination.

After a stretch of blustering, horns and traffic we have finished the pancakes and arrived at a lane of French-style houses opposite a park. A sign advertising space to let hangs from the gate into the complex, which is watched over by two guards. In the street, a man is peddling jackets set up on a clothes rail. I select a black leather affair. This will do.

The seller holds up six fingers. I hold up one. Wishful thinking again?

The seller shakes his head, feigning disgust. I shake my head back. He holds up five fingers. I hold up four. We give each other a firm look. I've never been good at haggling and besides, I'm freezing my tits off. I give in and hand over a few red notes. Just as I am putting on the jacket, a Mini Cooper pulls up.

"Miss Rose?" calls a spry man not far into his twenties, jumping out of the car.

"Why, yes!" Rose becomes coy all of a sudden.

One minute she's a wee girl. The next she's more grand dame. Well, a minor personality disorder makes for a more interesting friend than most. I'll give her that.

"Nice to meet you. I'm Speedy," the young man says in self-taught English, shaking her hand but not bothering with mine. "This way, please."

The guards block us at the gate. Peering from me to Rose, their mutters are peppered with the word *laowai*. After a bout of cajoling from Speedy, they eventually let us past.

"They said that your hair was like fire," he says to me. "They don't have any other *laowais* in the complex, so you're causing... how you say… a stir."

The lane is populated with what must have once been family homes for the well-off but have been split into individual flats. A couple of kids skip with a rope. Laundry hangs from bamboo poles. As Rose saunters ahead and Speedy admires her shape from behind, I ask him what *laowai* means.

"Foreigner. There are two characters," he says, pausing to jot them on his pad. "Separately they mean 'old' and 'outsider'." I like this, what with being an outsider anyway.

When we get to the furthest house on the left, which has a number six hanging from a nail on the door up the steps from the basement flat, Speedy gestures to Rose to go on ahead of him. He then realises that he is the one with the key and ferrets in his pocket for so long a blush spreads over his cheeks. He opens the door and leads us to the first flat on the right.

"It used to be servants' quarters," Speedy says, unlocking the door and regaining his composure.

The room has scuffed walls and high ceilings. A stained double mattress is shoved in the corner. A clock hangs from the picture rail by a piece of rope. Beside the clock is a glass door into a space with a sink and a bamboo chair. Next to the chair, a stepladder leads to a split level.

"The second bedroom," Speedy says, pointing up the ladder. "Can't fit two people up there at once though."

The ladder creaks as Rose makes her way up. "I think I'll take the downstairs, if it's all the same with you," she calls as I peruse what might be our new abode. Looking around, I notice that the cornicing has yellowed, as though several thousand cigarettes have been smoked in here over the course of generations. Home sweet home.

The ladder wobbles underfoot as I ease myself through the tight hole. Yes, the only reason this could possibly be described as a bedroom is because somebody – a marvel? a magician? – has managed to fit a bed into it. A single mattress is given privacy by a fly-curtain hanging from the roof. Past the bed, a divider splits the sleeping area from a desk and chair.

When I get back down, Speedy is staring at Rose with the attention of a puppy freshly delivered to his new owner. I'm glad to be able to stand up straight again.

"Can we toss a coin?" I ask Rose.

She fumbles in her pocket for a *kuai* coin. Tosses.

"Heads," I say.

She catches it, slipping it onto the back of her hand. It's tails. Of course.

"Yes!" Rose crows.

Fair play to her.

"There's another room for you to see," Speedy says leading us through the main hallway. A waft of frying onion and meat comes from the other side of a faded orange curtain hanging over the door-frame of the neighbouring flat. Speedy jangles with more keys.

"It's what I like to call a kitchen-cum-bathroom," he says. I'm impressed he can keep a straight face. A pipe pokes out of the wall at about head height, which seems to serve as the shower. A blackened gas hob sits in the corner. Several loose wires hang close to the toilet. Well, a hint of danger will certainly add excitement to wash time.

"For the sake of this," Rose waves her hand regally around the kitchen-cum-bathroom, all swagger. "Care to knock a bit off the rent? For us nice ladies?"

I have just seen, in actuality, Cupid's arrow enter Speedy's heart.

"Ten percent discount?" he says.

Rose looks at me. I don't foresee any great culinary efforts on my part. From having known her for nearly a day, I sense that she won't be for pulling the domestic goddess routine either.

"Done," we say, in unison.

*

Half a day passed. The top of the tree was still so far away that the caterpillar didn't think she would ever get there. Further down the trunk, she could see a group of ladybirds marching in a line. "They're all so lovely," she thought, admiring their polka dots. "I wonder if they'll notice me?"

Four

I decide to take the upstairs room to be charming and romantic, as opposed to how I am sure some might see it.

How some might see it: a shite hole.

I bang my head at least a dozen times until I learn to move around hunchbacked. Thus hunched, I set about arranging my life again. In the cupboard under the desk I find a black and gold enamel antique sewing machine. I put it in the corner. Makes the room more 'rustic'.

I wonder if China has TV home makeover programmes which invariably feature a blonde quixotic type butting heads with a more practical handyman? Almost without exception, these collaborations result in a design featuring stars stencils and pastel colours. I suppose I'm better off without.

I take out the notebook that I've had since I was seventeen. The dirty notebook. Perhaps this is the room in which my mind meanderings might take a clearer route. I scribble down a note about the plot. The main problem with the plot right now, I have to admit, is that I don't have one.

But perhaps that should be the point. The plot is not the point. Plotlessness should be the point. Surely?

On the shared courtyard below, the neighbours from the basement flat are stir-frying vegetables over a wok. One catches my eye from the window. I give him an awkward wave.

"*Chifanlema?*" he calls up.

"*Ni hao!*" I shout back, not understanding. Cloistered communism.

I manage to crack my head only once on the way to the stepladder. Downstairs, I find Rose erecting a floor-to-ceiling mirror next to a portable clothes rack. She adds plug-in vanity bulbs to the mirror and upends the rest of the contents of her suitcase. The selection of clothes ranges from nearly naked dresses to sensible business suits. I bet she's one of those sensible packers who balls up their underwear and puts it inside their shoes.

"Alexandre's having a party!" she says, attempting to de-crease a slip of silk with her portable steam iron.

"I don't have anything to wear." Nothing that isn't a stinking summer dress. Jesus, I'm more of a *girlie girl* than I realised.

"How about this one?" She selects a slashed purple effort that wouldn't be out of place on the strip in Las Vegas.

"Maybe." I'm relieved when she replaces it on the rack. I pick up the book resting on her pillow, *Making Your Mind Beautiful* by Dr. Phil Timmykins (M.D.). The pages are annotated and several passages are underlined in red pen.

"That book changed my life!" she says. "You have to read it."

My fringe obscures the words on the page; I blow it out of my eyes.

"Where are the nail scissors? I need a trim."

I reach for one of the four cosmetic bags resting beside her mirror. As I rifle through, she pulls it away from me.

"What are you, eight? Go to a hairdresser. What's the big deal?"

"I don't need to go to the hairdresser." I try to take the bag back.

"Yes you do!" she says, holding it out of reach above my head.

"No I don't!"

"This is the weirdest argument I've ever had," she says. "And I've had a lot of odd friends."

"I'm scared of hairdressers." I hang my head at the admission.

"Let's talk about it." Rose says, patting the corner of the bed. With legs crossed and head bowed, she channels mid-morning chatshow host.

"I was seventeen," I start, joining her. "It must have been July. I went for what I thought would be a simple cut. It was a different place to the one I usually went to. A friend I had been hanging out with at the time recommended it."

"Are you still friends with this person?"

"We don't really keep in touch since she joined the Ordo Templi

Orientis. I should have seen the signs when I first saw Brett. The tattoo of a parrot on his right forearm. The denim dungarees. The oversized glasses he didn't need. He kept talking about post-punk and using phrases like 'the new season'. I just agreed with everything because I didn't know any better. And in the end," I wince at the memory, "he gave me a mullet." Rose's mouth twitches but she admirably contains her amusement.

"Well, you look like a fucking hipster. Too busy listening to shoegaze on your iwhatever and wanking into your navel to... well, get a haircut."

There are worse things in life than being a hipster. Surely?

I've just about convinced myself when Rose interrupts with a killer blow.

"It looks like you're being ironic."

*

Jay Jay, the junior stylist at *Boom*, hands over a bunch of magazines to help make my decision easier. I set them to one side without looking.

For alternative amusement, I brought *Making Your Mind Beautiful*. Trying to dispense with cynicisms, I open the book.

"Chapter One: The Fruits of the Forest

On days when you question everything, consider the multifarious nature of the fruits of the forest. They are as varied as they are beautiful. Even if your neighbour appears to be an apple, does it mean that you should also try to be an apple? Pleasure in each other's differences is one of the great joys of life. Some days you meet apples and some days you meet oranges."

Rose has underlined the 'apples and oranges' part. While I am pretty sure that literature retains the power to spiritually enlighten the great unwashed, I suspect that anything Dr. Timmykins has to say will not. I close the book.

A hand taps me on the shoulder from behind. It belongs to a dude with a splendid mane spilling from his head. The cavalry has arrived. The dude introduces himself as Jimmy with a Cockney twang and ushers me to the cutting seat.

"What do you have in mind?" he says.

"I want it exactly the same, just a bit shorter."

"It's a bit overgrown, isn't it?" He runs his hands through the back. "I haven't seen a redhead for ages. Have you thought about layers? You know, all the big stars are doing this really lovely variation on the classic bob and…"

"Exactly the same," I interrupt. "But a bit shorter."

Jimmy's eyes drop to *Making Your Mind Beautiful*, now clenched in my right hand. He itches his chin in manner of a plumber about to attempt work on a serious drain blockage with nothing but a wire coat hanger and rubber gloves at his disposal.

"Well, all right, it is your hair," he concedes.

After shampooing, relations between us thaw. Jimmy tells me about his time training at a salon in London and we debate the merits of Dalston (Turkish food, charity shops, the market) as well as its downsides (six month waiting lists for cafes where you go to hang out with domestic pets, roommate interviews so intense you might as well be arranging a marriage).

"I loved it there. I came back to Shanghai because my girlfriend got pregnant and she wanted to be near her family. It's home but I'm not excited by it. It's better from a distance."

Communism with Chinese characteristics: smash-and-grab development and endless competing contrasts. How is that not exciting?

"Are you trying to find work?" Jimmy changes the subject.

"As long as it doesn't require me to kowtow to anyone and it's cash in hand. And it's not TEFL." Anything but TEFL.

"Fair enough. I might know of a gig in a club. A new one, see. Free for all. They want to get foreign people to go there. So they're recruiting foreign people to go there in the first place and party to make it look like the sort of place that other foreign people might want to go and party. But pay for it. If you see what I mean."

"Is it hostessing?" Images of girls who disappear in Asia only to turn up hacked into itty-bitty pieces a decade later spring to mind.

He shakes his head but my bullshit detector has pricked up. He does the 'mirror-from-behind' thing.

My inward celebration at the non-hipster, non-ironic hairdo is slightly undermined when Jimmy presents me with the bill.

*

Rose is bopping around to punk and wearing the steamed piece of pink silk when I get back. I grab a towel and head for a shower in the kitchen-cum-bathroom. In the shared hallway, our neighbour is hammering at the wall for no particular reason.

During my brief spell under the dripping tube that alternates between scalding hot and freezing, I see four cockroaches stroll from behind a loose tile on the lower portion of the cubicle. The last of them dislodges it completely.

Closing the door of the kitchen-cum-bathroom behind me, I trap my towel. This results in an unavoidable flash of my lady parts in the neighbour's direction. The guffaws elicited from the neighbour cause a small boy, presumably his son, to poke his head out from underneath the orange curtain before I can cover my bits.

"*Baba!*" the son screams, apparently terrified at the sight of a giant semi-naked white person.

As they shrink away in horror, I scuttle towards the flat.

"I've got you something to wear," Rose shouts over the din of the music, handing me a black dress. It's straps and vavavoom. Not my usual taste, but I don't have taste anyway. I guess this is what sexy looks like to most people.

"I've got a casting tomorrow," Rose says excitedly, glancing up from her phone. "TV show. It's called *Sex and Shanghai*. Listen; 'In the sexiest city in the world, one guy is about to find out what being in the pearl of the Orient is all about'. I'm going for the hot roommate of the main character who he has a crush on but is too scared to tell."

The immediacy of theatre is apparently forgotten in the face of immediate opportunity.

"Ah, that old chestnut," I reply, donning the dress and reviewing my now much more acceptable head. When I look at Rose, I instantly feel deflated. Still, it's fun to have gorgeous friends. They often have more outrageous stories.

"Well, if you become a star in *Sexy Shanghai*, don't forget me." I put mascara on and reach for the vodka and tomato juice. Fixing the drink, I substitute the local canteen's special sauce for Tabasco and cucumber for celery. The effect isn't altogether terrible.

"Sanguine Mary?" I hold a sample of my invention in Rose's direction.

"*Sex AND Shanghai*," she corrects me, breaking into a spontaneous dance. "All this restless energy. Don't you feel it?"

Tonight, tonight. Where will we end up?

*

We are both jiggered on Sanguine Marys and speed by the time we leave the flat an hour later. The path to the metro station takes us through Xintiandi. New Heaven on Earth, indeed. An enclave of Western-style shops, gift wrapped and populated with wild-eyed tourists in need of home comforts and Chinese with more money to burn than most. Wired punters stream out of the uniform coffee houses, clutching frappucinobabbinos as though they are the elixir of eternal youth.

Bohemia: forgotten.

In the bowels of the metro station there is a skirmish of pushing and shoving when our train pulls in. Rose rises to the occasion and gets her elbows out, eventually securing two seats at the far end of the train where we can continue our accelerated conversation.

A sour smell of alcohol mixed with sweat wafts through the carriage. It takes a little while to register that it's coming from the unconscious man on Rose's left. The other passengers – even those with masks on – cover their mouths in disgust.

Two stops later, the man is jolted awake by the train. He rubs his eyes with one hand and with the other grabs the bottle of water Rose is holding. Whipping it away, he drinks the whole thing. Rose taps him on the shoulder. He ignores her and deposits the empty bottle on the ground, closing his eyes again. Rose starts on a rant, partly directed at the man and partly a performance for the rest of the non-understanding carriage. I put on the internal radio until a very important question springs to mind.

"Shall we take booze?" Rose stops in full flood.

"I suppose."

I check in my pockets. My last eighty *renminbi*. Enough for a couple of packets of cigarettes, a bottle of rice wine and about four street food dinners. Rose rummages in her purse. She has a twenty.

"We could get a shitty bottle," I tell her. "Shitty bottle is better than no bottle."

"In this case no bottle is better. Let them think that we didn't have time in our busy schedules to buy anything."

"But isn't it rude?"

Rose assesses.

"I'll let you have that," she says.

Manners: vital for effective social climbing, it seems.

*

Alexandre's flat is concealed from the road by a security gate.

"Do you have business here?" the guard asks us from the cabin, in perfect English.

"Party business," Rose says. Totally legitimate.

The guard gives Rose the once over and pushes a button to open the gate. On the other side, his assistant escorts us to a building at the far end of the group of high-rises.

As we wait for the lift in the lobby, I notice that the assistant is armed. Unease prickles through my gut. The assistant shepherds us into the lift and presses the 'Penthouse' button. Rising, rising, rising. The unease dissipates when we arrive at the twenty-third floor.

Alexandre greets us with a smile that is probably induced by stimulants. There must be at least forty people draped around the open plan living area. Most of them are suits with local girlfriends. Rose and I are the only *laowai* females. Alexandre gives us to a brief tour of the flat, which is decorated in white with antiques scattered about. No mass-produced Nordic furniture in sight. I like the man more and more.

Alexandre and Rose step out onto the veranda. Taking the chance to ditch the panic-purchased bottle of *Yim Soo* that I believe may have originated in South Korea several decades ago, I head for the kitchen. I hide it behind the French plonk, gin and vodka and help myself to a Chardonnay from 2003, which has a hint of elderberry and citrus.

Faced with all unknowns in the living area, I make for the grand piano to attempt the one tune I can confidently play; chopsticks. Dededededededududududududu Didididididideedeedeedeedee.

And repeat.

A man comes over and starts playing the octave above. When we finish a couple of rounds he offers his hand and introduces himself as Jerome, launching into a spiel about his career in marketing. He talks so much my Chardonnay vanishes quickly.

When we go back into the kitchen for refills, Jerome reaches for the *Yim Soo*.

"Who the hell brought this?" he says.

"Terrible," I reply. Jerome hands me a well-mixed gin and tonic.

For the next hour, our chat is amicable until Jerome brushes his finger over my collarbone. I don't know why he would ever think there was anything sexy about touching another person's collarbone uninvited. There really isn't.

"You had a hair there," he says. "It must have come from your head."

"That would be logical," I reply, before I can stop myself.

I hope Jerome doesn't think that he has a chance. He's at least three inches shorter than me. I make my mouth move and other words come out, saying God knows what. Jerome asks for my phone number.

"I don't have a phone," I tell him.

"Ok, what's your address?"

This being the only type of situation in which I am efficient, I excuse myself to the bathroom, pronto. I stay in there long enough to examine the entire contents of Alexandre's cupboards. The most exciting items are a jumbo packet of condoms in an XXL size, which bodes well for Rose, and a recently prescribed rash remedy. Which doesn't.

Jerome must have given up hope. When I open the door, however, he is waiting patiently on the other side. He's dogmatic. Probably excellent at marketing.

"I'm going to find my friend," I tell him. Standard get-out-of-jail-free card.

On the veranda, Shanghai takes on a lustrous quality that I haven't seen it wear before.

Jerome has fallen away. If he comes back, I'll take inspiration from Alexandre and tell him I've had an issue with the terribly contagious rash on my vulva. Or any other STD to that effect. Yes, I reflect, looking at the changing light, there's always a Jerome. Or a Pierre.

Addendum: There's always a spare.

After I have hobnobbed with a few of the suits, despite having nothing in common with any of them, Rose and Alexandre find me. Both of their pupils are so big that only a sliver of the iris shows. Whatever they have been at in the interim, I wouldn't mind getting in on it.

"Rose tells me you're a writer," Alexandre says, the words coming out faster than his mouth is able to keep up.

"Not an actual, proper one," I reply.

"She showed me her work. It was great!" Rose babbles.

She will probably tell us that Mao was a really nice guy next.

"No I didn't," I reply.

"I want to read it, whatever it is," Alexandre says.

I want to read it when it's done too. Which will be…

Never.

*

It must be the next day and could be approaching lunchtime when I peel myself off the veranda, where I have been protected from possible frostbite with a blanket. Bottles and fag ends are scattered all over the wood panel floor. A discarded pair of knickers lies beside a potted Bonsai tree. I reach under my dress. They're not mine. That is a good thing.

I locate my handbag at the piano, next to where Jerome has passed out in an armchair with the bottle of *Yim Soo* at his feet. Several lines of whatever was bought last night are cut and abandoned mid-snort on top of the mantelpiece. I roll up my remaining fifty *renminbi* note and snort one. Fuck it. I snort the remaining two. The snorting causes Jerome to stir in his chair. Don't wake the beast, don't wake it. I leave on tiptoe.

A blue cab is pulling away from the carpark when I come out. Flagging it down, I try to make out the address scribbled on my hand, now smudged beyond recognition. I get in anyway.

"Just. Please. Drive." My voice is croaky from excess.

The taxi driver turns to me with the weary acceptance universally expressed by cabbies driving trashed punters home.

"*Shen me?*"

Where the hell am I going again?

*

The caterpillar watched the ladybirds pass her by without so much as a second glance. As their chattering faded away, she looked down at her body. It was as brown as the branch she was resting on. Blending in was a blessing, but wouldn't it be fun to have everyone's attention, like the ladybirds?

"One day, I will be beautiful," the caterpillar vowed, looking after them. "If I can only get to the top."

Five

I send my resumé out to try and swing a job, and thus feel like I am responsible when all evidence suggests otherwise. I can eat for two more days and then I'm really screwed. Being balls to the wall is my only real motivation at this point. I wonder if I will ever get tired of getting by on the skin of my bare arse cheeks.

Current condition of skin on arse cheeks: chafed.

I get one response: copywriting for a pleasure-aid company. I turn the phrase 'beggars can't be choosers' over in my head as I pick out an interview outfit from Rose's wardrobe. I try to imagine what a young woman who writes copy about sex-aids would wear.

"Embracing the clichés head-on, I see," Rose mocks, lifting her head from the bed as I spray on perfume, dressed in her PVC trousers and stilettos. "Do you think you'll get freebies?"

I let the question linger as rhetorical while I rummage in my make-up bag, selecting a beaten-up sample blusher in *Flirtatious Vermillion*. I guess if I'm going to be writing about penises all day, real or plastic, I should probably look like I've seen one recently.

"No idea." God, I'm nervous.

"You should negotiate it into your contract," she says, running a hand through her hair as she drags herself out of bed.

"What are you doing today?"

"I've got an audition later. Ophelia." She pulls a morose face in the mirror.

"You don't seem very happy about it."

Checking the time, I realise that I have to be at the place in about fifteen minutes. I have the brief but obligatory "haveIgotmypurse-bodyspraylipstickfagscash?" dither and dash around grabbing things. Rose continues to examine her reflection.

"Who's ever happy to play Ophelia?" She says.

I let her have it.

*

Outside, the trees are naked and the chill of the winter has temporarily lifted. I mentally run through the utterances one is obliged to wedge into any interview circumstance as I fast-walk along Wulumuqi Road through the former French Concession.

I am organised. I think outside the box. I pick things up quickly. I'm technically savvy. I'm a team player. I'm a team player. I'm a team *fucking* player.

The *One Is Fun* office is a shrine to fake cock. Clear cabinets surround the reception, filled with vibrators every colour of the rainbow. The receptionist, who introduces herself as Leaf but whose nametag says 53020, invites me into the seating area. Muted music videos play on the TV screen. A nameless girlie band. They're SHAKING IT.

The PVC trousers squeak as I cross and re-cross my legs, trying to remember the last time I used a vibrator in the unlikely event that it comes up. I always felt faintly stupid pressing a button to get off when there are boys out there to do it for me. I won't mention this. Although maybe it indicates a willingness to delegate responsibility.

Leaf starts to dust the wares. As I cast my eyes over the various shapes, ranging from pocket size to what could be an instrument of medieval torture, a balding man in his forties exits an adjacent door shaking hands with a go-getter with slicked-back hair.

"Thanks for coming in," the go-getter tells the man.

Well, at least I should be able to score points on comparable sex appeal. How grossly unfeminist.

The go-getter with slicked-back hair comes over to me.

"Stephen. Owner and Managing Director," he says, pumping my arm with the firm handshake of the self-made man.

In the interview room, Stephen spins me the history of *One Is Fun*; from the lowly days when they only stocked twenty varieties of knob to the giddy heights of 2005 when they were on the cover of *Hot Action* magazine, to the difficult years during the start of the financial crisis. I watch the clock above his head.

"Do you have any questions?" he says, when the seemingly interminable introduction is over.

You're always supposed to have questions.

"What are the opportunities of advancement in the company, should I be successful?" I ask, after too long a pause.

Stephen eyes me suspiciously and slurps on his espresso.

"We'll see. *Should* you be successful you will be responsible for writing the descriptions for all our pleasure aides. You'll also write press releases for whenever we create a new product."

"Great!" I loathe myself.

He pushes his open laptop towards me.

"I'm going to give you ten minutes to write a press release for the *Stocky Rocky*, our newest addition to the hugely popular *Wild Maid* range," Stephen says. "It's a test."

I pick up the *Stocky Rocky*, which has studs running in vertical lines from base to tip and at least twelve inches long. Now, that's just greedy.

"I'll be back shortly," Stephen says, closing the door behind him.

I get half way through before I realise that it's coming off as taking the piss and start again, making the prose neat and factual. I read it over. It's not terrible. I have a minute to go so I dither with the font, selecting one that is about as erotic as they go – wavy *l*'s and things like that.

Deciding it was better before, I press escape. The page goes blank. I press the back button. Nothing. I press it another four times. 'Internal Error' flashes up on the screen, which goes black and then revives. That can't be good. I press the 'escape' button ten or more times. Nothing. I hold down 'eject' until a CD entitled *Pan Pipe Your Way to Success* pops out of the drive, but nothing else happens.

Stephen comes back in and asks me to show him what I've written. I could tell him that I did write it, but because I am a Luddite with computers, I managed to delete it all. As I open my mouth it occurs to me that any explanation of my not understanding how to get back the now non-existent press release undermines the claim on my resume that I am Highly Advanced at Computing. Capitalised. As a moral compromise, I don't say anything and instead turn the computer around to present him with the blank screen.

"Where is it?" He scrolls up and down.

"There." Come on, brain. Think. "It. Is. There."

He raises his eyebrows and makes a tick on his clipboard. It's a fairly malevolent tick. I'm guessing I may well not be offered the job. How will he get me to leave without telling me that I'm a complete idiot?

"Thank you. We'll be in touch."

I inwardly applaud him for this elegant, though unoriginal, way of doing it. He even manages a smile. I get up.

"Before you go," Stephen says. "A suggestion. You'd make a better first impression if you weren't dressed like a nineteen seventies porn star."

I loathe Stephen.

*

Dejected, I wander through Xintiandi not quite sure what to do for the afternoon that is both free and fun. All the bars and restaurants are packed with yuppies. Oh, brave new world that has such *Starbucks* in it.

I watch a prepubescent boy wearing a traditional coat and with a bowl haircut play the flute in the south recess. The music soars the listener over the daze of the day, but there is only change in the gold hat placed at his feet. The other passers-by don't pay much attention.

"Yo!" comes a lazy American drawl from behind me. "Stop getting in my frame, please!"

The voice comes from a Chinese cameraman holding a video camera. Broad-shouldered, he has an unusual head of curly black hair, black eyes and a lean body that stands over a foot above my head. For a fraction too long we hold each other's gaze.

33

Nature of gaze: heated.

I duck away in the direction of home as the boy's tune ends, conscious of the cameraman's eyes boring a hole into my back with an electric charge. It's too much.

*

"You would have hated it anyway," Rose says, lying prostrate on the sofa as I release myself from PVC horror. "You're a poetic soul. You're too good for that shit."

I'm so touched by this comment that I let Rose's subsequent ramble about Alexandre, who hasn't called her back since *Yim Soo* night, wash over me.

"What makes him worth the energy?" I ask.

Ever the diva in turmoil, Rose struggles with the question. I let my mind wander. Who is worth the energy?

"I like his… hair," Rose explodes.

"And his independent wealth?"

"And his conversation!" she laughs, throwing a magazine at me and missing. "Ophelia went well, by the way."

I climb the ladder for a much-postponed writing session. Yes, hardy linguistic toil in my garret is the perfect thing to offset any feelings of worthlessness brought about by this most recent failure.

I settle at the desk but the blank pages of the notebook mock me. I watch a burst of rain instead, soothed by its rhythm. After a long time, I pick up my pen to write the first thought that springs to mind.

Freedom is often confused with carelessness. Perhaps they are not so very different.

*

I was sceptical about going to the effort of having a flat-warming, seeing as pretty much the only people we know in Shanghai are each other, a couple of French roués and a Chinese Opera academic. I have to hand it to Rose, though – by eleven o'clock, hoards of trendily dressed people I don't know have taken over downstairs, several pairs of high-top sneakered feet are hanging from the stepladder and sounds of someone being sick in the kitchen-cum-bathroom filter over a music mix that was thrown together at the last minute. A modest success, then.

One of the few faces I recognise belongs to Jimmy the hairdresser. Quickly smitten with Rose, he suggests we both punt for the supposedly-not-hostessing gig.

"It's legit," Jimmy says, as I dole out Loafer's Sangria.

Loafer's Sangria: wine you would otherwise not drink disguised with various juices.

"It might not be that bad if there's two of us," Rose says.

"We won't have to touch old men's genitals, will we?" I ask, unconvinced.

"Probably not," Jimmy says, handing us both luminous green business cards with *Straw Dogs – For Shanghai's Best Evening* printed on them.

"Ask for Michelle. Tell her it was me who put you in touch."

"Do you get a cut?" I ask, half-joking. Jimmy can't meet my eyes.

"Of course he gets a cut," Rose says. Alexandre chooses that moment to make his entrance, flanked by two anonymous suits. Pocketing the business card, Rose makes like a huntress.

"Is that her boyfriend?" Jimmy watches Rose and Alexandre hug. "Lucky bastard."

"It's a guy she's shagging and can have a conversation with," I tell him. "But I wouldn't go so far as to say he's her boyfriend."

*

Jimmy leaves at one o'clock in the morning, which is traditionally when the night should be hotting up. After seeing him off, I partake in the grass that is being passed by an apparently generous photographer called Gao Ming. His girlfriend Yvonne says nothing but smiles like Mother Earth at all times. A suit comes up to me.

"Where is Alexandre?" he asks.

"He's probably doing with Rose what a boy and girl have been known to do after drinks at parties. Shall we leave them to it?"

The suit looks at me like I'm the Antichrist and trots outside.

Super bromance: the ultimate turn-off.

Deciding I should to do as a good host and help him find his buddy, I locate the suit in the hallway smoking and muttering in French with Alexandre's other friend. For them, this must be the ultimate in slumming it.

"Is there a party?" a voice asks from the courtyard. I turn around. The cameraman from Xintiandi is hovering with an uncertain expression on his face.

Sounds of revelry drift from the flat. Behind me, Gao Ming is now playing an *erhu* accompanied by a bongo player, a spliff poking out of the left corner of his mouth.

I always hate it when people ask questions with obvious answers. It's hard to know how to reply to them without coming off as condescending.

"Well, yes. It's not a commune or anything," I reply.

"Redhead. I've seen you around."

"Not sure." I play it nonchalant.

"Xintiandi. I was filming. You were watching Xu Li."

"You told me I was getting in the way," I reply flatly.

"It was a cover. You distracted me."

"That's a bit smooth."

"I know," he says, grinning as he walks towards me. "I'm normally very bumpy, so it was a surprise for me as well."

I glance at the cameraman's feet. They are at least a size thirteen.

"Did you drop something?" He says, following my eyes.

"No, no. I just hadn't noticed the stonework before. It's beautiful."

He looks at the tatty cement without comment.

"Shall we?" I cock my head towards the door.

"After you."

We do the verbal dance as we make our way to the bar, an old bit of shelf we found and shoved on top of stray bricks. His English name is Roman, and he is a filmmaker and photographer.

"I chose Roman because I had a thing about ancient history when I was a kid," he says, embarrassed by his own geekiness. "My real name is Hsu."

"My real name's not Ruby, either. How is your English so good?"

"Watching American television and then living in San Francisco," he says. "I came back here to figure out what I wanted to do with my life. I still don't know."

"Sounds familiar."

Finding the Loafer's Sangria now has unholy green crystals floating at the top, I pour in more wine and give it a stir.

"You want?" I offer Roman a cup.

"I think I'll have a beer," he replies, half-smiling and rifling through his bag.

We stand next to each other but don't say anything for the length of a song. I ignore the residual acid sensation that goes along with the consumption of Loafer's Sangria. Roman doesn't stop looking at my face and hair. Self-conscious, I try to figure out how to position my body in a way that conveys that I am relaxed. It doesn't work. I give up and adjust the music on the stereo; a fail-safe for the socially awkward. Love's *A House Is Not A Motel*.

"I love this album!" Roman says.

The tension broken, we wander towards Gao Ming who has abandoned the *erhu* to skin up while the bongo player continues unaccompanied.

"Who was that boy you were filming the other day?"

"Xu Li? He's the subject of my documentary. He's gonna learn the flute from one of the masters in China. The master wants to teach the legacy of the art to a player before he dies and he doesn't have children."

"I'd like to see it."

"I can show it to you. But I was thinking lately that I should do photography again. That was my first passion. I fell in love with my model and it didn't work out, so I stopped. It's a bit of an old story. You could pose for me," he smiles, shyly. I don't know how to respond. There's too long of a pause. "I should go," he says, "I have to meet my

37

assistant."

In the hallway, we find Rose running her fingers through Alexandre's hair between bouts of kissing. As we step around them, I notice that it really is well-maintained, strong hair. I remonstrate with myself for being so cynical about her interest in him.

Roman tears the paper from the inside of his cigarette packet and scrawls a phone number on the white side.

"I'm not very good at making moves on girls. I haven't done it sober for about a year."

"I think if you said that, it means you are making a move." I take the paper.

"I am."

"I accept your move. I will make my move back later. What were you doing for the past twelve months?"

"Sleeping with people and not calling them again, for the most part. But I wouldn't mind changing all of that. See you."

I watch him walk all the way to the gate, until his shadow recedes. Slipping the paper into my pocket, I regain my senses and rejoin the party.

*

In the distance, the caterpillar could see a group of twisted shapes illuminated by a purple glow. The unknown excited her, but it seemed so different from what she knew of life from the forest. Should she keep trying to get to the top of the tree or go there? The caterpillar didn't know herself – how could she know what was the best? And there was no way she could manage to get to the far away place alone. Was there?

She hadn't even looked behind her yet and she was already confused.

Six

Rose and I hover by the cloakroom at *Straw Dogs,* waiting to meet Jimmy's contact, Michelle. The ostentatiousness of the pink leatherette couches and silver walls is only partly disguised by orange disco lights. One level up, an empty gallery overlooks the dancefloor where a few teenyboppers drunkenly motion to Europop. A group of lads with unfathomable amounts of gel in their hair groove past the cloakroom, livening the place up a bit.

Over the phone earlier, Michelle had assured Rose in broken English that this is the 'best decision you girls are ever making.' Whether or not this is true remains debatable.

"Jesus, I'm depressed," Rose says, looking around. "I didn't get *Sex and Shanghai.* Then last night I dreamt I was performing the *Vagina Monologues* at the Guildhall Theatre. And now this."

Here we go.

"Sorry about *Sexy Shanghai.*"

We watch the lads order from the burly bartender, who looks shocked at having something to do.

"*Sex AND Shanghai.*"

"*Sex and Shanghai.* But at least you had a good dream. I don't dream about anything."

"No, it wasn't good. I was naked. Then my mother showed up and started heckling me. I think it might be related to my latent subconscious anxiety. And my mother issues. It's all in *Making Your Mind Beautiful.*"

"I could have told you the thing about the mother issues. Don't read any more *Making Your Mind Beautiful.* When it gets too much, you should drink until you can't think anymore or go and hit golf balls. Or fire a gun!"

We are interrupted from the shit-shooting by a woman with punky hair and too much purple eyeshadow.

"You must be Rose and the other one," she says.

"Um, yes," Rose replies.

"I'm Michelle, Associate Social Event Organisation Partner for *Straw Dogs*." The woman holds out business cards that are identical to the ones Jimmy gave us except for her name and the preposterous job title.

"Follow me!" Michelle marches us to the left hand side of the dance floor past the stage, where staff members are selecting a backdrop. At the end of a passageway, behind the door marked Management Office, Michelle hands us contracts within thirty seconds of buttocks having touched faux leather. A child-sized Buddha on top of a bookcase looks over a pot-bellied man who smokes weed while playing solitaire on a desktop computer.

"All you need to do is hang out and make it look like you're having a good time," Michelle says. "Or, have a good time. And be nice and friendly to the customers."

"No genital touching?" I ask.

"What is *genital*?"

"Doesn't matter," Rose says. "It's a deal."

The contract is in Chinese and English; the translation has mistakes all over the place. While there is a time to get anal about these things, now might not be it. Clauses include number five, 'to dress proper, pert and attractive while on duty' and my personal favourite, number twenty-two, 'to clean body with adequate provisions for smelling pleasant at all times'.

The man ditches the butt of his joint. Checking us out, he puts his coat on and waves goodbye to Michelle. She waves back with a smile.

"That guy is laziest bastard in world," Michelle says, as soon as he's left. "But he's the boss's cousin."

"I didn't realise nepotism extended to the back rooms of clubs," Rose says.

"Nepotism making the world go round!" Michelle replies.

It's a beautiful thing.

"You can start your shift now. Let me show you what is what."

The main room is still relatively empty with perhaps forty punters in total. On the gallery level, a group of Russian dancers with complicated hairdos are changing into costumes in full view of everyone below. Dry ice merged with fag smoke creates a cloak of smog as thick as a Shanghai morning during rush hour.

"If you want to take a break I recommend the fire escape," Michelle points past the DJ booth to where the large red *Exit* sign glows. "But watch out when DJ Seven is playing. After he finishes shift, he likes taking girls back there for banging."

Fair enough.

The bartender, thrilled that Rose is still in attendance, sets a jug of orange liquid in front of two stools.

"Vodka and squash is the only thing on the house," Michelle says. Rose rolls her eyes at me. "Anything else?"

Bar fly duties: do not necessitate questions.

"I think we're covered," Rose replies.

Michelle struts off to the opposite corner of the club where a security guard is lurking and engages him in an intense conversation. Rose dishes out the alcohol.

"*Ni hao piaoliang!*" the bartender tells Rose. "You beautiful!"

The lads with unfathomable amounts of hair gel turn to locate the source of the bartender's admiration. Must be what I've privately nicknamed The FFE – the Foreign Female Effect. Rose takes the attention with her usual charm, enjoying every second.

As the uriney vodka and squash takes the edge off, the pop blasting from the speaker system mixes into a military march. The Russian dancers with complicated hair, answering a call to arms, stampede down the stairs from the gallery. It's *their song*.

"To the greatest night of our lives!" Rose shouts over the din.

The dancers jump on stage. Lackeys in the wings sporadically throw tinsel and stars as they gyrate, strobe lights obscuring their facial expressions. Hips, arse, attitude. The male punters stare at the dancers. The female punters stare at the men staring at the dancers.

Human zoo.

*

I'm washing my hands in the bathroom a while later when a young woman pushes past and pukes into the nearest sink.

"Are you okay?" I ask as she slumps on the floor. She takes a couple of deep breaths and tries to push herself from the ground. I pull her up by her arms until she manages to stand straight, wobbling a bit on her heels. She leans on my shoulders. I walk her through the bar.

A yellow cab pulls up just as we stagger outside. I manoeuvre the girl into the passenger side and close the door.

"Do you know where you're going?"

"Yes."

Scrambling to open her purse, she hands me her card through the open window.

"I'm Jia Ma," she hiccups. "Call me anytime. This is very good of you."

The card has an address, but no business name. As the cab pulls away from the curb, I make my way back past the bouncer. I nod at him like I did on the way in. Nothing. I smile. Nothing. His stoicism makes me want to bring him out of his shell even more. I smile harder. Still nothing. Bored with the game, I leave him.

Inside, Rose is ensconced with one of a group of male models that, according to Michelle, are regular fixtures. His name is Ashok. Rose told me she thinks that he can get her work. From a separately conducted conversation with Ashok earlier, I know he thinks Rose can get him work. I wonder how it will play out down the line as I make for the *Exit* sign.

*

The caterpillar had never known what hunger felt like, this ache inside that she had to satisfy. She stopped caring about the city or the treetop; looking at them did nothing to drown out the din that her stomach was now making. Picking up a leaf, the caterpillar licked her lips. With an indelicacy she was sure that the parade of ladybirds would disapprove of, she put her mouth to the leaf. She ate and ate and ate. It was as though a chasm had opened up inside her. Finally sated, her stomach bursting, she slept.

Seven

I arrive at *Bian Lian*, the Sichuan restaurant where I arranged to meet Roman, half an hour after the agreed time. I remember Rose's earlier "treat 'em mean, keep 'em keen" lecture. But perhaps this is going over the scale of being fashionably late to rude.

The buzz inside is an anecdote to the desolate street. The walls and furniture are all pine or pine-effect. As we hug hello and I shuffle out of my coat, it feels as though we've wandered into a sauna, except one with provisions for fried seafood. Bowls of shrimp with cashews, braised aubergines in black sauce and spiced cucumbers are already cooling beside beers on the table.

"I ordered," he says, apologetically. "The show is about to start."

We've just settled down when fast-paced opera music pumps around the room and a dancer in an azure mask bursts out. Twisting his limbs every which way, with a flick of his hand, the azure mask becomes red. Theatre flames pop from the floor.

"*Jia you! Jia you!*" the crowd cries.

"What are they saying?" I clap along.

"More!" Roman shouts. "*Jia you! Jia you!*"

The dancer whips his hand over his face again and the red mask turns pink. As the cheers gain momentum, the dancer's contortions become more elaborate.

"More! More! More! *Jia you! Jia you!*"

With a high-kick, the dancer's mask changes for the final time, to white. There is a brief interlude of calm, then the roar of applause. The dancer takes his bow. The crowd go back to their seats and smart-phones are returned to pockets.

After the meal we walk for a while, sharing secret ambitions. Even the lulls in conversation don't seem loaded. When Roman talks, his features soften and the skin relaxes at the corners of his eyes. His rough jaw-line and dark eyes stir a heady attraction. I try not to stare at him in the shadows cast by the streetlamps.

"I'm great at making friends," he is saying of his time in America. "But I'm not so hot at keeping them. Rose sounds like a good friend for you. Even if she is bat-shit crazy!"

"Hey!" I swat him on the arm. "That's my one friend in Shanghai you're talking about!"

We reach Zhongshan Park and put our bodies close to each other. I should leave now with the anticipation still in the air.

"My flat's near here. I know a decent rock place nearby," he says. "We could get another drink or two."

The chemistry has indicated that if we end up on a session, we may well end up having sex. While this wouldn't be a bad thing – in fact, it would be very good thing – it shouldn't happen because acting on lust now may jeopardise the longer game.

Libido: disagrees with all rationale.

"Would you like to meet again?" he says, sensing hesitation.

"I would." It's so simple.

At the top of the steps to the metro, I look back. Roman is still in the same spot watching me.

*

Around seven am, I'm at my desk in Rose's silk dressing gown. About a hundred cigarette butts are squashed into the jam jar next to the baggie of whatever Rose and I purchased at *Straw Dogs* to stave off boredom. Nobody tells would-be writers about the warped relationship with days and nights, so often propped up with alcohol and stimulants.

Forty scribbled-on pages are spread over all over the available surfaces of the room. These vary significantly in quality and legibility, but I can guarantee that a maximum of two will actually be any good.

Despite these endeavours, I still don't know what the plot is. Or where it is going, either. I glance over one; zero originality. I fight the urge to screw it up into a ball.

As the ladder wobbles underfoot, I try to bear in mind what a more experienced writer friend once told me; "Ninety percent of what you ever produce is crap, the other ten percent is just less crap." They should put that in the writers' handbook.

Handbooks: generally produced by 'experts' who haven't done that well themselves. I'll put that down to one of life's ironies.

I find Rose surprisingly awake and holding a damp towel to her head.

"I'm depressed," she says.

Not again.

She might benefit from the tough-love approach. Now is a good time to try it.

"You genuinely can't have developed depression between last night and this morning."

"A malaise, then."

"What?"

"Like an Edwardian lady. Me and Alexandre. He doesn't want commitment."

I flip through a stray fashion magazine filled with bones and pretty garments.

"I told him that my longest relationship had been six months. He trumped me though – his has only been three. He thinks it's getting too heavy already."

"Heavy like air?"

"As if he knows me."

Drawing the makeshift curtain made out of safety pins and old pillowcases, I catch sight of a butterfly flying past. Perhaps I imagined it.

Taken over by a sense that I don't quite understand and transfixed by the idea of the butterfly, I dash into the hallway where the neighbour from behind the orange curtain is sweeping up rubbish. I run past him, determined to see it again.

There it is, hovering by the white sheets on the washing line. I admire the delicate way it doesn't attach itself to anything; the intricate black, red and white patterns on its wings.

Disturbed by my presence, the butterfly flits off and dissolves into the metropolis.

Inspiration. This is it.

*

After twelve hours of non-stop writing, I bury the hangover with a dab of speed and go to meet Rose at *Straw Dogs* for another night of entertainment-slash-masochism.

Writing hangover: renders aptitude for normal functioning close to impossible.

Rose has been to three castings, had her hair done and is much merrier than this morning. But as we shiver under the *Exit* sign during the first of our many breaks, she has thought of another thing to complain about.

"I mean, what are they, the Gestapo?" Rose says.

"Who are they, exactly?"

"The government."

Despite the electrifyingly cold temperatures, the first and probably only guffaw I will ever utter escapes my lips.

"I can't believe they blocked my blog," she continues. "I had a decent following on *Hoi Polloi Toi*."

Rose doesn't care about the news or freedom of speech, but she does see any limitations placed on her internet audience as a step towards Dubya Dubya Three.

"You should know about this stuff. Don't you have a blog or a vlog or a website?" she asks. "Twitter, Facebook, Weibo?"

"Not my bag." Besides, what would Orwell say?

"Everybody else does it."

"Everyone else also thinks that probiotic yoghurt is different to normal yoghurt."

"You can have that," she concedes.

"Probiotic yoghurt is not any different at all."

"Fighting the good fight," Rose says, before switching her soapbox

47

back to freedom. "The more you have the more you want. It's like not seeing the end, once you've started. It's being boundless, it's floating."

We are both now filled with cheap booze from a job in a foreign country, yet in which we have both found the essence of our own particular freedoms. I decide to embrace it for what it is. It ain't going to change on my watch.

Pasha, the leader of the tribe of dancers with complicated hair, is having an altercation with Michelle by the dancefloor. Michelle doesn't look worried despite the fact that Pasha is at least a foot taller than her with a face so orange from overindulgence on the sun bed that she could pass for a blood relative of the Oompa Loompas.

"You say you pay me in a month, then another month, then another month!" Pasha shouts, "You pay me now or I walk! I take the girls with me!"

From Michelle's face I can tell she doesn't give a shit if she never sees Pasha or her troupe again. Still, manager to the core, she offers platitudes and hands her a few rolled up notes. Pacified, Pasha walks away, counting. Another day, another few hundred *kuai*. As the old saying doesn't go.

*

When Rose slips off with Ashok later, I take the scenic route home. As I weave past the temple, in the shift of the rising dawn it is a garish reconciliation of Shanghai with being Chinese. A hat-tap to a forgotten era that will soon be erased.

Not far from the temple, there is another construction site; the skeleton of a new behemoth. Inside the foundations are bunks where men are getting up for their morning shift. One prepares rice porridge beside a row of bedpans that lines the wall of their temporary bedroom, their pink flower decorations the only colourful element of the arrangement.

The cars start to populate the spiral of the overpass with more frequency. As I reach the lane that leads to the flat, a figure lurches into view.

Pausing beside a shack, Roman takes what he must think is a sly piss. As he zips up, he catches sight of me.

"You!" Roman hollers. "Of all the back alleys in all of Shanghai, why did you have to…" He stops. "I can't remember the rest."

"*Casablanca*. Badly quoted."

Roman follows my eyes to the side of the shack, which is covered in scrawled phone numbers.

"They're either for sex or fake electronics. It's really what China does best. Jesus, I'm drunk. You should be, too. It's a Friday night. What do you usually do on a Friday night?"

"Whatever normal people do. But I just finished a shift."

"What job finishes at five in the morning? Other than stripping or the factory line which I'm guessing, as a white girl about town, won't be your thing."

I hold my hands up. "You got me about the stripping." There's no way I'm going to tell him the truth.

"It's hard to tell when you're joking. Why don't we take a walk? My studio is close by. We can crash there," he says. "I'm not gonna jump you."

A few blocks away, opposite a Xinjiang restaurant, we reach a warehouse. Roman pulls the padlock apart, flinching as the door groans open. Through the dark, I make out several white boards dividing the warehouse into sections. Inside the squares, unconscious bodies lie on tatami mats or in tents directly on the concrete floor. Roman flips a switch and a portion of the sections is illuminated.

Half-finished paintings, bongs, paintbrushes, mannequins and other trash-treasure mark the trail to his section, which is decorated with photographs ranging from human-sized to polaroid. Other than the pictures, there is a plastic box, a bag of clothes and a mat.

I crouch on the box as he picks up his camera and takes a few snaps of my feet. "Come, here," Roman says, lying on the mat.

Fully clothed, I arch my back into him as he drapes his arms over me. For the moments I remain awake it seems natural. There is no sex in it. We sleep, curled and dirty.

As we make our way from the Yu Gardens along the Bridge of Nine Turnings the next day, the populace oozes through the confined spaces, impatient to see a display of fireworks that is happening later. The combination of masks on faces and snaking pathways would make anyone senseless.

Roman stops by a trinket stall covered with bracelets, charms and rings – nothing out of the ordinary. We're about to walk away when the owner holds out a piece of flat jade. I take it. It is about the size of my palm. While it is not very fine, the grains are clear and it has an inscription on the back.

"Garden of The Golden Valley," Roman translates. "Stories of passion make sweet dust, calm water, grasses unconcerned. At sunset, when birds cry in the wind, petals are falling like a girls' robe long ago. It's Du Mu."

"Pretty words," I say. Roman pulls the stallholder aside.

"*Wei shen me, na me gui*?" Roman haggles. Eventually they agree a price. Roman hands the piece of jade to me.

"Thank you."

Even through the window of the bus we jump on to escape, the smog seems to penetrate our skin. On the other side of the Waibaidu Bridge, what was the British consular building is a remnant of a curious era where the Empire was top dog. It's a hotel now.

"Where are we?" I ask, nudging Roman in the belly.

"I'm not going to tell you." He takes my face in his hands and kisses me, drawing mutters of disapproval from the old biddies behind us.

All the moves I would previously have scorned are now the most perfectly expressed sentiments that a man could utter. I kiss him back.

On falling in love: enjoy well before sell-by date.

*

The element of water moulded the thing that was once a caterpillar into another shape. A version of the earth moved inside her. Opening her eyes, the thing that was once a caterpillar surveyed the walls that had formed around her while she had been sleeping. The thing that was once a caterpillar wondered what was happening to her. Where the metamorphosis would end.

Eight

Jia Ma waves from the other side of Lujiabang Road. As I cross, I narrowly avoid colliding with the nearest moped driver. She looks a lot better than I remember. The wide-open face gives the impression of generosity, stopping short of homeliness by the impishness of her eyes.

"I want to buy you a dress,' she says. "To say thank you for helping me."

"You don't have to."

"I also want to say welcome to China! Besides, a woman's life isn't complete until they commission their first *qipao*."

The market is a cross between a warehouse and a shopping plaza. Reams of chiffons, silks, satins and leathers scatter every available surface; blazes of colours and textures are given away cut-price. Stallholders yell the new wave hello and hold out their wares.

"I used to be an English translator but I'm starting a business," Jia Ma says, as we go up the escalator. "It's a café, like the ones from the fifties in America with jukeboxes. I always had a fascination. I can't think of a name, though."

One floor up, Jia Ma leads me to a tiny woman at the far end who is hoisting a roll of fabric onto her shoulder. "Di Di was a friend of my grandmother's. Nai Nai used to have a stall upstairs that sold buttons for years before she passed away."

Di Di picks her way up a ladder positioned beside a precarious stack of materials. She heaves the roll from her shoulder onto the top of the stack. As she descends the ladder, Jia Ma catches her attention. Smiling, Di Di murmurs to Jia Ma in Shanghainese.

"She said you are like a fox," Jia Ma translates.

Di Di shows us a look-book of re-imaginings of the classic *qipao* form. Here mini-dresses, there full-length gowns. Each page also presents various styles of collars, sleeves and lengths. Concentric patterns, flowers, hopscotch embroidery. A world without corners. How safe and warm this lady is in her sphere, where everything is aligned and soft. I briefly envy it.

"These are her designs?" I try to keep the surprise from my voice.

"She had a good job for a long time in a multinational. She gave it up because she didn't get to meet the women who wore her clothes."

When Jia Ma shows Di Di the shortlist, she interrogates our choices, looking me over closely. Evidently this is a more serious process than I had first realised. They debate solemnly for half-an-hour during which time I mentally redraft the third chapter.

"We think a traditional style, simple and classic," Jia Ma announces. "What colour would you like?"

There's a blue in the far corner. One I've only seen in isolated Scottish landscapes. A blue that doesn't have a bottom. That's my blue.

Di Di hoists the roll down and holds the corner up to my cheek, nodding in agreement. After she takes my measurements, Di Di produces a camera from her handbag.

"She doesn't see foreigners much," Jia Ma says, embarrassed.

I put my arm around Di Di and smile, a phony film star. The camera clicks and flashes a few times. Satisfied, Di Di lets us go.

"Come by and visit the café next week!" Jia Ma says as we brave the maze. "It'll be all ready for you. Don't forget!"

*

When I get back to the flat, I find a note from Rose.

Gone to Beijing for a few days with Ashok (!) Merwoman 4 in 'Merwoman's Revenge'! I get a line!

In the spirit of celebrating a good day for all, I go for a nightcap. Giving my now habitual wave to the guards, I stop to buy cigarettes from the man at the corner shack. His daughter, a toddler, is trying to help him fix a microwave in the back. She giggles when she sees me, hiding behind his legs.

"*Baba, laowai!*" she says, peek-a-booing between his calves.

At our local jazz dive, *Insomnia*, brass tones from the players punctuate the punters' conversations. After an hour I'm sizzled on mojitos and pondering whether or not I should give up the idea of the novel and join a band.

Pros of joining a band: allows for travelling, irresponsibility and the consumption of Class As on a regular basis if desired.

Cons of joining a band: inability to play any musical instrument, keep a consistent rhythm or hold a tune may prove a drawback.

Conclusion: definitely worth considering.

A man with a coat hanger for a body quivers beside my table. He introduces himself, holding out a golden business card. *William Orange, Creative* it says. I turn it over, expecting to find an elaboration on the back. Nothing.

"What does it mean?" I ask the man. "Creative?"

"I have ideas."

I wonder what my potential business card job description would be. Loafer?

An equally rail thin woman in a fur hat embraces Spindly William from behind. It doesn't look all that comfortable.

"Darling!" she says to the back of his head.

The saxophone player makes his way to the wings. The woman in the fur hat turns to me. Close-up, I remember her face but not her name. Rollo? Rizla?

"Have ve met before?" Rollo-or-Rizla asks, her voice a mixture of Russian staccato and Valley girl upward intonation. "You have blonde friend? She is actress?"

"Rose?"

"I came to the club you work. You don't remember?" A smile crosses Rollo-or-Rizla's face. "Vat a character! And vat a funny thing to be doing with yourselves! Do you know, William, that this girl and her friend do hostessing at that terrible bar we went to last week!

Like the Shanghainese whores! Isn't it *hilare*?"

Spindly William obediently laughs. I could tell him how funny I think it is to have a career that is really an adjective. I decide not to. Fishing around in her bag, Rollo-or-Rizla hands me a flyer with *House of Rika* and a picture of a girl in what looks like a bin liner on it.

Rika! Bingo.

"For my new fashion collection. You must come! Bring ze actress! Bring all your friends!"

"I'm not sure what my schedule's like." Like I have a schedule. Gathering my handbag and jacket, I leave without saying goodbye.

Outside, I lean against the wall, strangely irked by Rika's comments. You can only go so far until your life becomes a series of escapes. You just have to hope that the present escape is better than the previous one.

*

The rooftop of Roman's warehouse studio looks onto the surrounding slums. I have been wearing a body suit and covered in gold paint for the duration of the shoot, which has been going for a couple of hours. I agreed to do it after heavy persuasion on Roman's part. I'm not regretting it. Although I haven't seen the pictures, yet.

An artificial coconut tree, the only prop, teases the sky. Roman's assistant, Amanda, runs forward with a make-up palette. Her hair flops over most of her face. Like most observers, it seems she wants to be invisible herself.

Amanda paints more gold on the ridge of my nose and eyelids. Pulling out her needle and thread, she sews the waist higher and tighter. I can barely breathe.

"Climb the tree," Roman says, adjusting the one lamp that has been set up. I take a swig of gin and perch my left leg on the trunk. How the hell did I get here? No. I should stop asking questions. That one in particular.

"This is your journey to the East. Remember that. You are the Monkey Queen."

Roman goes for so long I lose any inhibitions and climb further up the tree until Amanda whispers to him in Chinese, interrupting the flow. When Roman responds with ill temper, I'm glad I don't understand.

"But I want to show her!" Amanda says in English, picking up the last roll of film from the table and avoiding eye contact with me.

"Go do it, then!" Roman replies, caustically. "Now you've said it!" Amanda climbs through the hatch back into the studio.

"What's she doing?" I drop down from the tree and take the cigarette from Roman's mouth.

"She's going to the dark room right now. She wants to develop the last roll herself. That girl, she's a crap assistant because she doesn't like to listen, but she's gifted. That's why I'm being harsh. I'll let her do what she wants for a while until she fucks up. If I'm too nice to her now, she won't be as good as she could be."

"How do you know her?" I take a drag and toss the cigarette over the edge. The cherry glows brighter then fades out as it falls, extinguished by its own weight in the air.

"She's a childhood friend from Xi'an."

Roman places the last lens carefully in order on the picnic table. He picks out another lens and mounts it.

"This will show your pores. I want to see your skin!"

With a flick, Roman hoists the old film out and loads a new one.

"This one is really out of date. Let's play with it and see," he says, winding it in. "As I was saying, Amanda will be so good that she'll overtake me soon. I hope she'll remember me!"

I'm back in position and Roman is figuring out his angle when Amanda reappears, brandishing a newly-developed photograph. It is the first time I have seen her look anything other than sullen.

"Good thing I just started!" Roman's sarcasm is biting.

Roman takes the photograph carefully and pulls her close in a celebratory half-hug.

"This is why you can actually learn from me, although I know you think you know everything."

"Can I see?" I ask.

56

"Of course."

He brings me the picture with a grin. Sure enough, there on the shining paper, is a fantastical golden version of myself I didn't know could exist. The monkey queen of a Shanghai that's hers for the taking. For once, my expression is victorious.

"Beautiful," he says.

*

The thing that was once a caterpillar had no control any more. A motion, a rhythm, was causing her body to shake and shift. Shake, shake, shake. It was relief and pain at the same time. A contradictory expansion that gave her to herself. She surrendered.

Nine

The words *House of Rika* are spray-painted on what resembles the interior of a space shuttle, which serves as the backdrop to a stage in the corner of *Beauty Bar*. The place is otherwise decorated with chrome-domed hair dryers and old-school barbers' chairs. Maintaining suspension of disbelief doesn't just apply to stories, it seems.

New rule regarding the attendance of parties, even if you don't like the people holding them: if there is free champagne, it's totally acceptable.

Rose's anecdote about her most recent gig, as an extra in a local period production, has been going full-steam since we arrived. Her efforts to get her face on camera were repeatedly thwarted by a girl called Jenny, who managed to jostle to the front take after take.

"We froze our tits off in a concert hall for four hours in twenties garb. And they gave us shitty food for lunch," Rose says as we head directly for the free champagne. "There was an oversight by the producer and they couldn't find enough foreigners to cover the space from the back. So they ended up substituting *laowais* for Chinese kitted up in blonde wigs. It was all a bit David Lynch."

Preppy kids, indie foreigners and at least two full-blown acid freaks are already diving around in the middle of the dance floor. I spot Roman setting up his camera by the DJ booth and shoot him a wave. He smiles. The buzz is on and the mood is high.

"Davide!" Rose exclaims, air-kissing a trilby-wearer in his mid-thirties who I quickly gather is Rika's French husband.

On Davide's other side is a woman with black hair who could be ten years older than me, although she may have just lived a lot. There is nothing soft in her panther grace.

"This is Veronica," Davide says.

"So happy to meet you!" Rose thrusts out a hand. Veronica's mouth twists in a semi-smile.

"Such beautiful laydeez!" Davide beams to the three of us. "I love you girls!" Handing us fresh drinks, he wanders off to meet and greet.

"I wouldn't normally be seen here," Veronica says with a lilt in her voice that I can't place. "But Rika is an old friend." She looks us over carefully, adding, "We can party together. I'll take you to all the good places."

Veronica takes Rose's number and wanders off to talk to a large man with a scar on his face standing at the bar. I cock my head at Rose in the direction of the bathroom and we exit post-haste.

"She's a big deal on the Shanghai scene," Rose says. "From Romania. I wonder who that guy is."

"How do you know this stuff?"

I cut a couple of lines on the top of the toilet cistern.

"Come on, what else are extras supposed to do on film sets except nurse eating disorders and gossip?"

"Touché."

I snort a line. I don't care what anyone says, drugs are marvellous. Apart from the come down and addiction parts. But let's not worry about that.

"Do you think I should have sex with Glenn?" Rose asks.

"The dealer? I don't think we're there yet, are we?" I wipe my nose and hand her the rolled up note.

"He's really nice," she says, snorting. "So smiley. So friendly."

"When I bought that, he gave me a really animated speech about how he was the rightful King of Abuja. He was so high that his pupils were blending into his skull. Golden rule of the occasional drug user; don't shag the dealer."

"I'm glad you're here to help me not make the mistakes that I would otherwise definitely make and instead make altogether different ones," she says, handing me the note back.

*

59

As Rika comes on stage from behind a curtain dressed in a catsuit crafted from purple lamé, I feel the less frequently experienced type of hubris that accompanies champagne and cocaine on an empty stomach for those of the confused egocentric bent. Shyness is overcome. I own the room. I *am* the room.

"It is vith great pleasure that I introduce to you my first collection as ze *House of Rika!*" Rika cries into the microphone. "Ze inspiration for *House of Rika* comes from my experiences vile meditating on ze human body and our place in ze space and time."

Davide gives a whoop from the corner. Those who are still sober enough to have full control of their bodily functions clap half-heartedly. Roman hovers beside the action, filming.

"I would like to also explore ze themes of musical energy and synergy in ze creative process," Rika continues, "So vith zis, I vill sing you song I compose originally in English."

Rika disappears behind the curtain. A pause. Everybody's eyes wander to the DJ booth, which seems to have been left unmanned. A sweaty guy with an afro pops up behind the decks. Rightly embarrassed at having missed what was probably his one cue of the evening, he hits a button.

As the introductory notes of Rika's theme tune trill from the speaker, I can only assimilate it to the funeral march as remixed by a four-year-old that is handy with an electric keyboard. She re-enters from the wings, now dressed in a silver foil ensemble.

"*Oh, vith zis future of ours,*" Rika sings, "*Vat can ve expect? Vat can ve e-x-p-e-c-t?*"

The audience, perhaps not expecting this, remains impassive. Bold as brass, Rika continues to the chorus.

"*Ve expect ze future! Ve expect ze democracy! Ve expect ze liberty!*"

The music is cranked up and models shimmy onto the stage. All of the clothes are variations on the themes of bright and foily. Once the last model has taken position, they start a can-can. When they reach the final few steps of the routine, Rika joins in. Lime green strobe lights and artificial snow compete for visual attention.

"*We expect ze future! We expect ze democracy! We expect ze liberty!*" the models sing in unison with Rika.

"If they keep saying 'democracy' and 'liberty', it'll be my ass," *Beauty Bar's* manager murmurs to another member of staff.

The music stops. A lull precedes the odd stray handclap from kinder audience members as Rika bows. There is a pattering of a collective movement of feet in the direction of the bar. By the curtain, Davide leans over Roman, drunkenly grabbing the monitor on his camera. Roman's face sours. As I make my way towards him, I am flagged down by Rika. I try to circumnavigate her but the place isn't big enough.

"You!" Rika squeals.

There's no getting away from the bony tentacles of the foiled body.

"Yes!" is all I can say.

"Vat did you think of ze show?"

I'm now going to have to lie in order to preserve her feelings. Or be honest and maintain what dubious integrity I still have. Fortunately, Spindly William butts in.

"Wonderful, darling!" Spindly William says as he embraces Rika, glancing at me with no hint of recognition.

Rika thus distracted, I seize the opportunity to avoid further interrogation about the alleged artistic merits of the aesthetic equivalent of a hit-and-run and slither off to Roman. On the dancefloor, Ashok is putting a cherry in Rose's mouth while a couple of his cohorts look on with glazed expressions. I'm glad she's being diverted from thoughts of Glenn the Dealer.

*

Roman's neighbours are playing *mahjong* when we negotiate our way through the lane to his home. As he chats with them, I realise my high has worn off.

"They said that you are a freak," Roman winks at me.

On the patio, there is a wooden table and chair set with curling legs that may have come from the Middle East. Inside, Roman switches the television on mute and goes off into the kitchen. A pile of prints mounted on thick white card dated from the previous year sits on the sideboard. Roman has signed them on the back. They are mostly of an elderly man in African landscape. In the last one, the man is shirtless and facing a stretch of desert peppered with tumbleweed. There are scars all over his back, the skin pocked with black and pink spots. Jagged lines are scraped on either side of his spinal column. Yet this back doesn't express defeat. With his hands up and open to the earth, he is a figure of strength as awesome as the scenery.

"I took them when I was in Zimbabwe," Roman says from over my shoulder. "They're left behind from an exhibition I had a couple of years ago. You can have one if you want." He holds out a gin and tonic.

I set the pictures back on the side table. He puts an arm around my waist and kisses the back of my neck.

"Can I show you the outhouse?" he says, into my hair.

Located through the kitchen's back entrance, the shack is decorated red except for one white wall. Antiques, knickknacks and curiosities line the room, including a collection of stuffed animals ranging from raccoon to duck. The quaintness is only undermined by a double-screen computer set on the desk and camera equipment tucked beneath it.

Roman fiddles with the projector. An image of Xu Li playing flute with an old man comes to life on the white wall.

"That's the master," Roman says.

The master plays his flute; Xu Li copies, but incorrectly. The master thumps the music stand and gives the boy a long lecture, slapping him on the head. Briefly, Xu Li's face breaks but he keeps it together. The next time it is better, but far from perfect. Each time Xu Li makes a mistake, the master scolds him at length. After fifty attempts, Xu Li's tune is lilting and seamless. When the master congratulates him, the boy's face doesn't crack a smile – it becomes harder. The scene fades to black.

Roman smells musky and distracting. He crosses his legs towards me. The chemicals can't be ignored. He takes my hand, lust making his face a dictionary of sorts.

"Shall we…?" I start.

We make it to the doorway when I realise I can't even wait to get to the bedroom. I turn and kiss him, pushing him onto the computer chair. His hands move under my skirt, his fingers exploring. I unzip his fly. As he goes in there is no pretence. I move slowly at first, slowly. Supple, shaping, we are a hand-stitched garment. Faster and faster. I move and move again. As we come, I forget I am a thing.

*

It's at that serene stage between late night and early morning when I meander home through the *longtang*. At Zhongshan Park, red and golden lanterns swing from shop fronts. In front, two elderly Mongolian travellers sell their wares, spread on thin black blankets. The jewellery is mostly silver twining interspersed with coloured stones. I'm quite taken with a ring set with a green stone. The woman, who has a pleasantly time-eroded face, holds up ten fingers. Handing over the money, I pocket it.

"*Xiexie*," they shout after me.

The rubbish collectors are making their first efforts at the crap scattering the pavement. A pine chair with a broken panel hanging from the underside is attracting attention. One of the rubbish collectors, evidently feeling that it might come in useful, deposits it in the front vestibule of their truck.

"*Laowai!*" He shouts at me, closing the door of the truck and reaching out to haul a bag from the public bin. This raises a laugh between them; the eternal joke of not being Chinese.

Foreigner. *Laowai*. Old Outsider. Old Eye.

I am a big old eye.

*

Checkered flaps of red, brown and black spattered with white pressed against the walls that had formed around the thing that was once a caterpillar. The wings pushed and pushed, overwhelming her senses. Thought

63

became flesh.

She shook out her wings and admired the pattern that adorned them. Taking a few steps, she let instinct guide her. The wings carried her away from the branch and above the grass.

So this was the transformation of things.

Ten

"Try it!" Jia Ma says, pushing herself away from the counter top. As the stool swivels in a circle, her hair flies over her face. I push myself off, too. Around, around, around.

Chuckling, I breathe in the smell of fresh paint from the walls of her café. The bright yellow is complemented by black and white checker tiles. Booths of dark red hold tables set with cherry blossom tablecloths, on top of which rest sauce dispensers shaped like over-sized tomatoes. She definitely has an eye. But still, a nagging thought.

"You can't call it *Starfucks*," I tell her, when the stool has ground to a halt.

"I want to say, 'fuck the man'," Jia Ma says, spinning faster.

"I don't think you can really say fuck the man when you're a fully-fledged small business owner." And dressed, head-to-toe, in fake Versace. "You kind of are the man."

Jia Ma stops spinning; the confused face of capitalism with Chinese characteristics.

The man: Similar to God, you don't necessarily have to like him but it's helpful to make friends for arse-covering purposes.

"You're right," she says, slowly.

"Am I?"

This so rarely happen that a warm feeling spreads from the base of my gut through to the tips of my toes.

"Can you think of anything else?"

She passes me a bit of paper and a pencil. I write the first decent name I can think of. A homage to the homeland.

"Gilded Balloon," she reads, "*Gilded Balloon*. I like it."

She jumps off her stool and ferrets beneath the register. At least it's a hell of a lot better than *Starfucks*. I light a cigarette. Yes, I reflect, she'll never fully appreciate how much better a name it is than *Star-fucks*. Jia Ma's head pops back up.

"For you." She holds out a brown paper bag. Inside is the fruit of Di Di's labour. Shaking the *qipao* out, I almost don't want to try it on. I have the feeling that any human contact will make it less perfect. It should be in a frame. Hanging on a wall. Not on my body.

In the storeroom filled with empty paint pots and discarded yellow rags, I slip the *qipao* over my head. I look in a stray shard of mirror that lies on the ground. It must be the cut. That's not me. The waist is tiny, the hips voluptuously exaggerated. The neck, swan elegant in the high collar.

When I step out to show her, Jia Ma blows a high-pitched wolf-whistle. She selects an Elvis track on the stereo; we break into a twist.

Life is now complete. Allegedly.

*

On a backstreet in deepest Suzhou Creek that evening, Jia Ma and I locate number 1455 behind overgrown bushes having walked past it four times already. The warehouse is brightened by posters advertising the expatriate theatre group's performance of *Hamlet*. None of them bear Rose's face.

A lightening flash from the event photographer's camera adds a necessary dose of prestige to the entrance hall, where an usher waves us up the spiral staircase to the front row of the audience of around a hundred.

"Feels good to be out of work," Jia Ma says, taking off her coat.

I'm about to agree with her, but then I realise that this is just my life. We look around the spectators; a mixed bag of foreigners and locals. A group of middle school kids have been dragged here by their headmaster, who looks on from the end of their row.

"Expats can do things here that they never would at home," Jia Ma says, jerking her head at a Western guy in his sixties being preened attentively by a local girl not a day over thirty in the row behind us. "Take them. Do you think he'd be with someone like that if he were back in Alabama?"

"What's in it for her, though?"

"Hello!" Jia Ma says, her accent mingling disconcertingly with LA-speak. "A visa!"

Darkness falls before I can reply. An actor runs out from the wings.

"Who's there?" he cries.

"Nay, answer me: stand, and unfold yourself!" A voice answers from far behind us.

*

Realising that the fall-out from this is not going to be pretty, I buy two double gins before heading to the green room. Best to go with provisions.

Downing hers in one does nothing to soothe Rose's petulance at a production that was saved from amateur dramatics by the talent of the actor playing Hamlet, an amiable Australian called Steve. Rose doesn't like Steve. One tiny bit.

"He had two curtain calls!" says Rose, outraged. "Two!"

"To be fair, he is… Hamlet," I say.

"Right before curtain up he told me not to start my speech too quickly after his exit on the 'get thee to a nunnery scene' because it ruins the moment. Patronising twat. And he hogged the dressing room as per fucking usual. I need sex or charlie."

The other actors have already departed the scene of the crime, save Rosencrantz and Guildenstern who, true to character, are sticking around after hours.

Jia Ma plucks up the courage to join us. Despite profuse apologies for her mobile phone ringing during Ophelia's mad scene, every attempt she makes to engage Rose in conversation is met with monosyllabic answers. Her gaffe apparently unforgivable, Jia Ma swiftly departs to an electronica night at a dance club, *Evil*.

"It's the right place for her!" Rose bitches. "In any theatre the audience should know god damn well to turn their fucking phones off."

Guildenstern, a Spaniard in his twenties, slopes up to our table. Rose continues, oblivious. "What are they? I mean, did she ignore the announcement at the beginning? No wonder they're fifty years behind the rest of the world."

"It wasn't that bad!" I pour a bit of my gin into her glass.

"It *was* that bad and you know it. I'm never acting again!"

"Thank Christ for that," Rosencrantz mutters as he puts his coat on. I decide that I can't take any more of Rose either and make my way out to see the lover, leaving her to the charms of Guildenstern.

*

Gaining speed and rising higher, she who was now a butterfly felt satisfied at the appreciation on the faces of the ladybirds watching from the grass below.

"Would you like to rest here?" the leader of the ladybirds called up from her spot in the eye of the sun.

"Yes, please," the butterfly replied, without hesitation. Why would she refuse?

The leader of the ladybirds shuffled away and the butterfly lay down.

"Beauty might be a very useful thing," thought the butterfly, as she spread out her wings to absorb the rays.

Eleven

A crowd of what must be hundreds has gathered outside the *Crown Plaza Cinema* for the world premiere of *Shanghai Spy*. Most of them are teenage girls who spill over the metal barriers erected around the red carpet. They scream with hysteria as our car pulls up. When we get out, their disappointment is quickly alleviated by the arrival of the French leading actor featured in the posters that have been plastered all over town for the past two weeks. A cacophony of screeches and mass appearance of smartphones greets him from the stretch limo.

The famous: filet mignon in a feeding frenzy.

Tottering behind Veronica and Rose in the seven-inch heels and mini-dress Rose insisted I wear, I watch the young girls grab the French actor for selfies, proclaim ardent love and thrust gifts at him. He takes it all in his well-chiselled stride, his model girlfriend left hanging.

Rose trots up the steps of the auditorium behind Veronica, gathering the hem of her full-length gown.

"I'm going to network the hell out of this evening," she says, the woes of Hamlet forgotten. "I'm more of a film actress anyway."

Rose's networking skills are becoming increasingly sophisticated. She has learned to ascertain an acquaintance's usefulness to her within about fifteen seconds. She first hits them with the spiel about her talents and experience that she doesn't know I've overheard her practising at home. This takes approximately forty-five seconds. A sprinkling of polite chat leads to the extraction of the business card. The whole process is usually completed in the time it takes to drink a glass of champagne.

At the VIP entrance, a security guard ushers us through to the reception area behind Veronica without comment. She barely spoke to us on the way here, instead spending the car ride having a long phone conversation in Romanian. As the pain of the shoes works its way from my ankles up, I debate whether or not there is a correlation between the height of heel one chooses to wear and the desire to increase one's social standing.

A gong booms over the gorgeous-people-chitter-chatter. "Guests, you are now welcome to enter the cinema for the screening of *Shanghai Spy!*" the tuxedoed host announces.

This is definitely a version of 'it'.

*

The afterparty is in a private members' club called *Love Bug*, located two floors above the auditorium. Madhatter's Tea Party cocktails consisting of cranberry, vodka and iced tea, are served in porcelain teacups. Veronica flits off to do the socialite rounds while Rose flirts with an American called Vincent. He's in movies. He thinks that he can get Rose a part in the movies. For tonight, at least, she's in love.

I decide to leave them to it and wander to the tank that takes up one stretch of wall, transfixed by the baby sharks inside. I barely notice the man on my left-hand side.

"Hello, again," he says, putting out a boxer's hand. A scar trails from the base of his chin into the top of his shirt. Where did I meet him? Oh dear. I never used to be that girl.

"You don't remember me from Rika's extra-terrestrial experience?" Before I can feign disagreement, he continues, "I'm Goh. We didn't speak, I just know your face. Did you like the film?"

As it was in French and had Chinese subtitles, I spent the duration mentally redrafting chapter nine and contemplating the size of the French actor's feet. I did, however, manage to pick up the key plot points. A male spy alternates between kicking arse, shagging various affluent women – age seemingly unimportant - and using improbably clever gadgets to explode historical monuments in a bid to fight terrorists, who are the only non-Caucasians apart from his geeky

70

Shanghainese sidekick. He wins. I think.

"It was challenging." Good answer.

"You speak French? What a talented woman! What did you think about the political slant of the story? Did you think it was a reasonable representation of China today? The translation lost the essence of the piece, in my opinion."

This being the first time anyone has ever told me I am talented – albeit for a skill I do not possess – I am not keen to enlighten Goh to the more humble truth. However, given that this is a predominantly French-speaking crowd it's likely I will be caught out later down the line if I lie.

"I don't speak French."

"You read Chinese?" Goh is even more impressed.

"No." Damn you, honesty.

"Ah." A faint smile quivers at the corner of his mouth. "Out of curiosity, what were you doing when the film was playing if you can't speak either language?"

"I was thinking about my art," I tell him, as earnestly as possible. It's at least forty percent true. Goh's smile grows into what has to be described as a smirk.

"And what's your art?"

I can feel the blisters forming on my big toe. "If you don't mind, I have to go to the bathroom," I say, hobbling away.

"Hope to see you again," Goh calls after me.

*

Padding through the assemblage of would-bes and could-bes later, I brush past Veronica.

"This is Joe," she introduces the man lurking on her right-hand side. Joe's rubber-tire lips remind me of a catfish. The French actor is ensconced with groupies and business people at the bar behind him.

Veronica notices my bare feet. "Are you crazy?"

"These things are ridiculous." I hold up the shoes as whoops of laughter come from the French actor's group.

71

"If you'll excuse me," Veronica says, heading straight towards them. Social decoy: me.

When I mention that I like to write, Joe stops scanning the room for more important people to speak to. His eyes take on the kind of intensity generally reserved for snakes watching a nest of baby birds. At the bar, Veronica is air-kissing the French actor into oblivion.

"I need a writer," he says. "What kind of stuff do you write? Is it commercial?"

"I wouldn't go so far as to say – "

"I'm a producer, I make movies," he interrupts, handing me a racing green business card. *China Adventure Movie,* it reads. "I'm working on a movie right now. It's a feature in post, *Going the Distance.* But I might need you for *Tree People*, which is in development. I have a lot of ideas for the script. I'm an ideas guy, you see. But I can't write."

*

Abandoned games of chess and mugs of strong brown tea decorate the path as I wander up Roman's lane barefoot. When I find him in the outhouse, he is editing Xu Li and the master's recent performance at the Beijing Theatre.

"That guy!" Roman says, laughingly, when I show him Joe's card. "He had to leave the States because he fucked over too many people. I think he's on the run for account fiddling. There's probably a bounty on him. Don't touch unless you're desperate."

My bullshit detector got it right.

"Tell me how you met Xu Li," I ask, looking at the screen where the boy and the master play.

Roman has rebuffed my more probing questions before so I half-expect him not to answer, but he freezes the concert and lights a cigarette.

"I went to talk to him after I saw him perform," he says, blowing a smoke ring that slowly dissolves. "He thought I was trying to buy his ass. He was terrified but he came off as if he would do it. I said, 'No, no, that's not what I want. I was thinking we can make a movie about

72

you and what you do, your journey.' His face lifts. He is so happy. Truly, I have never seen anyone so happy. He didn't even remember my name, but he hugs me very hard and he tells me a Mongolian proverb. I forget now which one it was, it's to do with luck. Well, from then, he's my buddy."

Pleased at the rainbow beam of this shared confidence, I pull him close.

"We met again a few months ago when I came back to China and he had been working with the master. He once asked me why I was always moving. He said it diminishes feelings. That boy, he wants to go one place and make it big. But I want to go to a thousand places. Is that spoiled?"

A thousand places to go: more chances of getting lost.

That would be kind of wonderful.

*

Keen to try out her new wings, the butterfly flew towards the city. The hub of lights and tapestry of mechanical noise overpowered the evening air. As the butterfly reached the edge of the mass of objects, she found herself in a state of wonder again. She flew faster, higher.

"From now on," she thought, "I will not stop."

Twelve

Set apart from the rest of Moganshan Road by a residential lane, the square footage of the gallery is at least the same as an aircraft hangar. It's nearly full. Even taking into consideration the proportion of people here just for the canapés, that's still a tidy amount of genuine interest.

The walls are hung with the series of Roman's portraits which bears the title, *Journey to the East*. Images of models dressed as classical Chinese characters flank the photograph of me, the Monkey Queen. To capture a face; anybody can do that. Freakish though they are, these magnify deep-seated vulnerabilities and longings.

Roman is hovering by the Tibetan band that volunteered to play, already flushed from wine and happiness. Amanda claps her hands.

"Friends, welcome to our Journey to the East!" Roman's voice strains to fill the space. Amanda translates in Mandarin. "This show could not have been possible without the help of my talented assistant who has worked with me, hour after hour, to make it happen."

Amanda lowers her head.

"And to the models!" A hand pushes me forward. The three other girls come out, equally bashful, and we absorb the cheers together. In the back, I can see Veronica standing with Goh and another friend, which does nothing to soften any self-consciousness. Here and there, I am congratulated by partygoers. The pseudo-celebrity is entertaining. If China made a model out of me, what could it do with a genuine beauty?

Nightfall brings 'sold' stickers to four of the pictures, including mine. The blue *qipao* glows in the eyes of the moon as Rose and I dance to the Tibetan band with a couple of older hippies. We are lifted with weed, red wine and good spirits. Veronica makes her way over with Goh and the other guest.

"What a show!" she says, warmly. Evidently I have now earned my stripes as a friend who is worth having. Rose holds out her hand for Veronica to join the dancing, but she doesn't.

"You!" Goh smiles at me. "Quite the girl about town, I see. You're friends with Hsu?"

"Roman. Yes, we're friends," I say. I don't know what we are.

"Roman, Hsu. A man of many names." Their faces are softened by the cosiness of the evening but it's still tricky not to feel defenceless under the strength of Goh's stare.

"We're on our way out, but congratulations again," Veronica says, turning to Goh and her other friend. "Shall we?"

I watch Goh walk away, detached from the surroundings for a moment.

"Let's get a drink," Rose says, with a shake of her hips, reaching for the ice bucket. A pair of hands grabs me around the waist. Roman.

"I sold your picture!" Without saying any more, he picks me up and spins me around.

"Excuse me, lovebirds. I need to go outside and vomit," Rose says, abandoning her drink and ducking out. Roman keeps spinning me until Amanda tugs at his sleeve, whispering in Mandarin. When he puts me down, she looks over the *qipao*.

"Strange to see that kind of dress on you," she says, amused, and turns to Roman. "We have to wrap up Cookie's portrait for Sisi."

"Be right back," he says, going off to the cellar with her in his wake.

*

By midnight, a sheaf of business cards swells Roman's breast pocket. We reach *Insomnia* to watch Theo, a jazz trumpeter from New York who is in China on tour.

"This guy bought your portrait," Roman says, holding out a business card as we wait at the bar.

Goh Fashion I read. "I spoke to him. He didn't mention anything about it."

"He might like to keep things private. It was the easiest sale I've ever had. I told him a bit about Xu Li and the documentary. He's interested in funding it. Only takes one fat cat to say yes and then they all join in. Or, if I can get him to sponsor another series of photography, maybe I can make it big that way. Maybe it will get my name out there."

Roman sticks out his hand to order drinks. His phone rings constantly.

"I said we'd talk tomorrow," Roman mutters, pressing buttons until the frantic sounds stop.

Two twenty-ish British guys in pull up stools next to me. One has a Scottish accent. It's the first time I've heard it in a long while and sounds lovelier than the melody coming from the musician. I close my eyes to catch it.

"What are you doing?"

I open my eyes. Roman is staring at me.

"Listening to their voices, that's all."

"Homesick?"

"A little."

When I hold out my hand, the barman trots over to me, ignoring Roman.

"You're drawing attention to yourself." The charm has evaporated into coldness. Roman picks up his drink and moves closer to the trumpet player.

Taken aback, I pay the barman and tap the Scottish guy on the shoulder. We start to blether. The American Dream cocktail has enough rum in it to slosh away any anxiety about Roman.

"Are you here alone?" asks the Scottish guy's friend, in a northern English accent.

"Oh no, I'm with him." I point to Roman, who keeps his eyes on the trumpeter.

"A Chinese fella?" asks the Scottish guy. Is that surprise?

"Yes."

The trumpet player finishes his final set to prolonged whoops from the audience. As the notes fade, Roman returns. While he normally gets pink about the face after alcohol, he looks drawn. Hungry. The lack of music emphasises the rage in his voice when he finally speaks.

"What makes you think that you can talk to my girlfriend like that, right in my face?"

"The lassie was standing there on her own," says the Scottish guy.

"What's the matter with you?" I ask Roman.

"Let's go," Roman says, finishing the rest of his drink. He bangs his glass down on the bar and wipes his mouth with the back of his hand.

"Are you okay going with him?" the Scottish guy asks me, sizing Roman up. Grabbing my wrist, Roman pulls me outside.

"What the hell was that?" I shout. Roman releases my arm.

"Those guys pissed me off, that's all," he pants, the adrenaline rush giving him colour again. "I don't like that type of guy."

Holding my arm up to the streetlamp, I can see the red divots where his nails were digging into my skin undulating under the light.

"You know, those are the kind of guys who come to China, date Chinese women and fuck them as much as they want because they're big white men in a foreign country."

"Don't make generalisations about things you know nothing about. They were nice!"

"God you're self-righteous!"

"Of course I am. But you're wrong anyway!"

I stick my good arm out towards the passing traffic. A cab stops straight away.

This could be it.

Me and him.

It.

"Tonight was everything I have wanted for a long time," he garbles as I start to get in. I stop half inside, my legs dangling above the gutter. "It all came at once. I'm sorry."

The driver, irritated, clicks his tongue. Unable to do public arguments with any kind of conviction, I go to Roman. He puts his arms around me. We stay there long after the cab has driven off without a passenger.

"Let's run away for a bit," I tell him, breaking the stillness.

"Where do you want to go?"

Just about anywhere.

*

"What a thing it would be to experience happiness," the butterfly thought, *as she raced with the cars moving on the road below her. "But what makes it possible?"*

The shapes of the city became clearer to the butterfly. Maybe there, amongst the sounds and the sorrows, she would find happiness.

Thirteen

The forecourt of the Shanghai Railway Station does nothing to indulge romantic notions of train travel in a foreign country. Bodies squeeze onto the pavement. Migrant workers huddle in a makeshift camp while they wait for a ride. For once, more are leaving the city than arriving, thanks to Chinese New Year.

Children run up to us as soon as we have stepped out of the taxi, mewling for money. As we push through the throng, I hand the closest boy a twenty *kuai* note. He runs back to his mother, who is waiting by the subway entrance. She picks him up and spins him around. This opens the floodgates; we are tailed all the way to the building by the others.

"I don't speak Chinese!" Roman tells them in his thickest American accent, pointing at me. "See her? We're not from here!"

Startled by his severity, the kids stop following us. Most of them move on to other potential targets. Those who return to their respective mothers with nothing receive squawks of admonishment for failing to have done their job properly. A security guard starts yelling at the mothers. The most imposing mother hollers back, then reluctantly picks up her blue and red checker bags and moves on with her little girl in tow.

Roman gets past security without a problem, but when I go through the metal detector I set the alarm off. After my frisking by the guard, we're late.

We run to the departure gate and just board the train in time. Multi-stories slide past. As the train picks up speed, the grey of the constructions slowly brightens. We weave through suburbs where houses pirouette from one other, as if reaching the final movements of a dance.

*

Our gondola meanders through the winding waterways of Zhujiajiao. Roman suggested this detour en route to Xi'an, our final destination. The streets of the town are populated with stalls selling wood-carvings and snacks of pork buns and cobs of corn. While I'm guessing it would normally be packed, only a few other visitors stroll through the twisting alleys.

"It's a tourist trap," Roman says, as the gondolier returns us to the mooring. "And about as close as I'll get to taking you to Venice."

When we get off an old lady accosts us, holding up a bilingual sign: *The Bridge of Setting Fish Free*. She points to the bridge behind her. Her cart, parked beside it, is piled high with bags of black and golden fish in water. "Buy fish, make wish," the old woman says.

Roman selects one fish bag and we climb to the middle of *The Bridge of Setting Fish Free*. Holding the bag together, we throw the fish into the water below. Roman takes a photo of me looking after it.

"What was your wish?" he asks, taking my hand.

"That's cheating."

As we walk back down *The Bridge of Setting Fish Free*, Roman stops to take pictures of the scenery. The old woman we purchased the fish from is now crouching beside the canal on her haunches, clasping a small net. She strains forward, her back arching in effort. Practised at this, she quickly catches something. Evenly whipping out a plastic bag, she puts the fish into it, adds water and ties it in a knot at the top. She then tosses the bag onto her cart with the others.

Noticing me, she smiles, the picture of innocence. I know that look; I do it all the time; so shameless I can't help but laugh.

Folklore or not, I still hope that it wasn't our fish.

*

On board the sleeper to Xi'an later, the squeeze is tight in the six-person berth that is otherwise taken up by a family. The top bunk is commandeered by an ancient man, presumably the grandfather, who shifts up and down the ladder with the dexterity of a circus performer. "All these people!" Roman, exasperated, struggles to put his bag in the storage compartment. I pull out my notebook and perch on the corner of the lower bunk.

"What are you doing?" Without waiting for my answer, he dives onto the bed and nestles into my arm. "Our first trip. Next time… who knows? Berlin!"

"Maybe." I flop my legs over him, the notebook abandoned. I haven't written a single sentence for over a week.

The train engine reverberates through the corridors and up into the nooks of the sleeping cars.

"I was there for a workshop a couple of years ago," he says. "Always wanted to go back."

"Why didn't you?"

"I'd need a job or a European visa," he replies, kissing the back of my neck. "I think Amanda will meet up with us when we get to Xi'an. She's home for the holidays, too."

"Oh." I wonder if the disappointment in my voice is as obvious as it feels.

"We were thinking about making another project with you, my little muse."

His eyes close.

From the train window the hills roll gently, flowing into one another. As the time passes, satellite towns give way to tea plantations. Men weave through the icy fields pushing wheelbarrows full of slop. Two hours into the journey, I notice a child rambling in bushes, not far from the train tracks. She stops dead, alarmed by the noise of metal on metal. I wave at her. She waves back. We hold each other's eyes until she vanishes.

*

Much later, sleeplessness leads me to the food carriage, which is deserted apart from a waiter whose eyes droop from his post behind the counter. In a booth, I watch the moving picture outside. It has now dipped into blue black, but there are still contours of hills merging with marshlands. Reeds from the murk below flank the exteriors of houses. The plants seem to support the structures more than the wooden legs on which they stand, their existence alienated from their essence.

Another town comes into view, fracturing the stillness. Half-built flats pepper the otherwise traditional style of the streets beside them; China stampeding towards its future as its past still clings tight. All this is done publicly and nakedly, as a snake sheds its skin.

The elderly man from the top bunk parks himself at the booth to the left. Opening a metal tea canister, he takes a sip and gestures to me. I smile and shake my head.

"*Ni shi shen me guo jia?*" he asks. I think for a minute. *Where are you from?*

Being a travelling Scot is a bind when you always have to explain that your country is neither in, nor part of, England. Or in London. Or in Ireland. Or an island at all. Moving over to his booth, I pull out my notebook and tear a page out. The man watches as I sketch out a Wellington boot shape, so astounded that he smacks his canister down and spills a few drops on the table.

"Scotland," I say, pointing to the top.

"Scot-lan," he mimics. "*Sugelan.*"

"*Sugelan*, Scotland." I reply.

"Scotland," he says again. "I speak good English!"

Conversation thus exhausted, he pulls out a pack of cards and shuffles the pack, flicking them back and forth. He holds out the stack.

"Shhh!" he says, as I take the top one.

Queen of Hearts. I place it face down on the table.

"Queen of Hearts!" he says, cracking a smile. He must do well with ladies in the post-menopausal market.

I shuffle the pack of cards. "Pfff," he exhales, unimpressed by my efforts. I split the pack in two, placing the first card face up. Ace of Spades. I point at him and he follows suit. Three of Diamonds. My turn. Three of Clubs.

By the time the sky takes on the black depth of the wee hours, the ancient man tires of the game and returns to our berth. His hand brushes my shoulder as he leaves.

"Scot-lan," he chuckles, walking back to the carriage.

*

When we disembark the train in the morning, the hubbub of the other passengers pushes us forward with a feverish momentum. I abandon myself to the tug of the crowd poking at my ribcage and pulling my hair.

Outside Xi'an's station, families await the arrivals of those they haven't seen for years. Reunions, embraces, slaps on the back.

What travel is really for: missing and being missed.

"Come on!" Roman pulls at my hand as we extricate ourselves to join the back of the taxi queue. Roman catches the heel of the woman standing in front of us with his bag. She can't be over twenty-one. Irritated, she looks from me to Roman and then at his hand clasped with mine. Picking up her bag, she walks forward, muttering under her breath. Roman, hearing, shoots back. The woman ignores him.

"What did that girl say?" I ask, as she slams the door to her taxi and it drives off.

"She called me a 'banana'. You know, yellow on the outside, white on the inside." I want to say I'm sorry. I suppose I don't really need to. Do I?

"Whatever," he says. "It's not like I give a shit what other people think, anyhow." He pulls his hat low over his forehead until it almost conceals his eyes.

On the drive to the hotel, the lines of the streets distract us from being the odd couple. The Bell Tower glistens as the cab moves within Xi'an's walls. To the left, the Drum Tower competes with its resplendent brother for attention. Still further left is a mosque, shrouded by the rising car fumes of the morning rush hour. Fighting against the uniformity of Xi'an's otherwise rigid layout, swarms of vendors peddle fireworks for the New Year's celebrations from their carts.

Located on the opposite side of town and outwith the walls, our hotel is on the same block as a bunch of new-builds but has the curling rooftops beloved of ancient depictions of the Middle Kingdom thrown together for the benefit of tourists.

"Why don't you live here?" I ask Roman as we make our way past the bellhop. He strides in front of me to the reception counter.

"It's never enough," he answers, ringing the bell for attention. "For me, anyway. I always wanted to get out."

*

The butterfly was amused by a light box hanging by the side of the road. It would flash green, amber and red.

"How strange people are," the butterfly thought, as the box changed from red to green and the cars moved away. "Letting themselves be told what to do by colours in a box."

As the cars diverged, the butterfly found herself at a crossroads. Not so much an end, but a beginning of sorts.

Fourteen

The bus pulls up at the entrance to the Terracotta army site, where the walkway is lined with security checks manned by guards. I can't help but feel as though I am entering a military base rather than an historical landmark.

We skirt the walkthrough that circles the first pit. The thousands of figures stand to attention. Despite his despotic ways, I have to hand it to Emperor Qin Shi Huang. It takes a hell of a strategist to rule one of the largest countries in the world and try to take the best parts of your empire with you to the afterlife.

Two young men behind us examine the warriors as they wait to get to our vantage point at the centre of the walkthrough. "Do you think they're real?" the shorter of the two says in New York brogue.

"I don't buy it," the second says, snapping away with his point and shoot nonetheless.

In a screening room, an educational video depicting the discovery of the site plays. Two peasant farmers in Xianyang Village are in the midst of worthy labour. One of them comes across a piece of the army. He beckons to the others. With gusto that undercuts any element of realism, other peasants gather and examine the faces of the Terracotta statues. They all instantly forget their lives of toil.

In case I forgot: history is made by winners.

*

We navigate our way through the Xing Qing Palace grounds to the lake that stretches across the panorama. Frost nips at the edges of the pathways that lead us past the Flower Shedding Brilliance Pavillion and the Dragon Tying Hall.

As we head for the boat mooring area, I indulge a fleeting fancy of this being a way of life always. Maybe the name, Xi'an, is to be taken literally. This is a form of heaven on earth. These are moments to be savoured, as transient and unrepeated as the movements of the lake.

"Race you!" Roman yells, tapping my shin with his toe and dashing off ahead.

"Not fair!" I call out, taking a grand total of ten paces before I realise that I can't really be bothered.

Roman untethers the fishing boat anchored on the farthest corner of the pier. He helps me on and we push off, holding an oar each. When we reach the centre, we stop rowing and let it drift. As we huddle together to watch our breath crystallising, Roman takes a swig from a hip flask and offers it to me. We inhale and exhale. His hand, resting on my arm, starts to progress under my coat and towards my right tit.

"It's freezing!"

Taking my left hand, he puts it on the now swollen crotch of his jeans. Apparently the blood circulation is going strong.

"I've always wanted to have sex on a boat." He kisses me on the cheek and pulls my sweater down to reach the collarbone.

There is nothing sexually inviting about our current location but this could be the reason I didn't wear underwear today. His tongue moves to my nipple, circling around it. With his right hand, he works his way up in between my legs. Well, only the fish will be able to see.

I undo his jeans, giving in to the wetness spreading from between my legs. His cock rises out of the gap. Too excited now, he stands up to take his coat off. The boat, not in favour of these shenanigans in what is a sacred place for contemplation, wobbles in protest. Roman loses his footing and lands in the lake. Laughing, I wait for him to surface. Nothing.

"Are you all right?" I call, as loudly as I can, holding my hand out. Should I dive in, too?

"ARE YOU ALL RIGHT?" A couple of air bubbles pop. Nothing.

Fuck. Fuck. What is it they say? "Unless they're blue in the face, they're probably fine."

"Roman?"

Suddenly, his body lunges out of the water. "Haha!" he hollers. "Who's laughing now?"

I'm still laughing, really, because I'm bone dry. I decide to keep this an inside observation.

"Fuck! Just… fuck!" he says, pulling himself onto the boat.

We manage to stop laughing and Roman rows us back, chastened. Perhaps like so many fantasies, when one is presented with the reality there is the inevitable man overboard and somebody ends up wet.

*

The streets of the metropolis were a kaleidoscope of neon and heat. The butterfly admired the figures of the people as they jostled for space, but their faces all looked the same to her. The butterfly paused on top of another light box.

"I hope I will learn to differentiate," she thought.

Fifteen

I've stumbled on an opening at a gallery called *Oi-O*. The display is mostly of digitally altered landscapes of outside Xi'an's walls. There are about ten people here, including the owner, a man in his forties with chains on his spectacles.

"This one," he says to the assembled group, gesturing to a picture of a derelict building where five children are playing with a skipping rope, "was torn down last week. I don't know what happened to them. But what's to be done?" The question lingers in the air as he goes to answer the ringing phone.

The three girls and two boys all have the dullness of skin that comes with malnutrition. In another country, the girl to the right would be on a catwalk in a few years. The price tag on the photograph says 500 RMB.

I make my way out of the exhibition just as a teenage girl removes the bars from a bicycle and runs off with them. At the end of the road, a young man is washing his friend's hair in a plastic basin. The young man tips the contents of the basin into the gutter. His friend stands up, his hair on end.

Leaning against the wall, I find a copy of *Madame Bovary* in my handbag. I open it at random.

"Do you know, Charles, why that clock strikes? To announce the death of another hour."

Roman arrives four chapters later.

"Ah," he says, noticing the book. "She gets bored with her husband and then kills herself. I think there's a love interest in between."

"She's one of my favourite contentious heroines! And you, my dear, are an hour late!"

"I had a meeting with Amanda about setting up the studio." He holds out his hand. "Come on."

At the crossing, a minivan swerves past us. The driver's expression suggests whatever is coming out of his mouth is probably not pleasant. In the back of the van several kids with filthy faces rest on top of over-full checker-patterned bags. They crouch low, their feet touching the oil slopping on the metal floor. The one nearest the back of the van is wearing a suit, sweater and trainers. No harm in keeping up appearances.

We stop at a fruit shop that has buckets of rotting produce parked outside it but inside is a veritable dreamscape. I point to one of the biggest red apples. The shopkeeper holds up five fingers.

"He's overcharging," Roman says, hanging back.

The shopkeeper sweeps the floor. Behind him, from the ladder that is fixed beside the rows of melons at the back, a leg belonging to a child dangles from what must be the loft. A cartoon theme tune wafts from above the leg. I open my purse.

"He's ripping you off!"

"It doesn't matter."

I hand the shopkeeper the money.

"They're gonna eat you, honey," Roman says, as we leave the shop and continue down the street.

"Eat or be eaten. Human nature."

At the park nearby, a group of elderly people practice calligraphy beside the frosted flowerbeds by the entrance. Frozen bamboo sweeps over the pathways. Visitors rest on benches, oblivious to what is going on around them and the cold. An urban idyll, in every sense.

We stop at a bench beside the main square. Roman takes out a tissue from his back pocket and wipes the seat for me. Elderly couples dance on a raised platform. They twist in circles, accompanied by drums throbbing with an offbeat rhythm. To the right, ladies wave red and pink flags. They try and fail to keep time with the wayward beats.

Roman pulls me close. He smells like clean man and pheromones. The sensory explosion is there.

*

The restaurant is red brick with open fires. The cosiness goes a good way to lightening up the doomsday mood I can't get rid of. It's probably a good thing Roman doesn't know my track-record of buggering up the familial meet and greet, soiled forever at the age of eighteen when my Catholic boyfriend, who had a dirtier mind than most, took me to meet his Mum in Moffat. I should have seen the warning sign when she kept bringing up Leviticus over the roast beef. Live and learn.

"Mama, papa, my uncle, his wife, their daughter," Roman says, his hand sweeping in a circular motion at his assembled family. "Nobody apart from my cousin speaks English so don't worry too much."

Roman's persona has changed to the good son and he chats to his father and uncle with the backslapping bravado that I thought was reserved for public schoolboys at Eton, circa nineteen fifty. Roman's mother and aunt stare at me. His cousin, who must be twelve, whispers to them.

I have never wanted a vodka and tonic more than I do at this precise moment. The waitress, however, serves tea and beer. The three beers are placed in front of the men. The women are left with the teacups.

"May I have a glass?" I ask Roman, pointing to the beer. His father and uncle watch me with unsure half-smiles.

"It might be better if you didn't drink too much tonight," Roman says.

"Why?"

"My family is quite traditional. Particularly about women and alcohol."

"Fine," I say, picking up the tea instead. Is it fine?

"I learn English at school," the twelve year-old interrupts my thoughts. "My English name is Little. We're so excited to welcome you to join our family, and to China."

"Welcome… where?" At the back of my head a red-alert bell is ringing. Meet the family, not join the family. Can I take this as part of the language barrier?

All eyes follow when I excuse myself. The night air is a relief. Lighting a cigarette, I take a long drag. I don't think I've ever felt as aware of either my own foreignness, or being female, as I do this evening. I'm not used to having to play at being the subservient miss.

On the pathway to the restaurant, a couple make their way to a parked car. The woman leans on the man, who helps her pick her way between the stones. Watching their progress, I realise I've probably been gone for as long as I can get away with. There's nowhere to hide, now.

At the table, Roman's aunt is having a deep-and-meaningful with his mother. I smile at them as they laugh together over a private joke. I wish I understood. I could do with a giggle.

As bowls of soupy noodles and whole steamed sea bream are passed around, Little leans towards me.

"Can I tell you a secret?" she says. "I'm bored."

"I can understand that," I reply.

"What do you do?"

"I work in a bar and I try to write."

"How did you meet Roman?"

"He was shooting his film."

"He took those photos, they were of you? I saw them. You're a superstar!"

"I don't know about that. What do you want to do when you're older?"

"First I will learn French. Then, I will go and study fashion in Beijing. Then, I will go and live in Paris. Then, I will start my own company," she says, with the clarity of one brought up in undeniable privilege.

Roman's mother embraces me when we gather in the restaurant car park after dinner. Pulling back, she looks me over again. "Beautiful," she says. There it is, that word again. I wish you could know me, I want to tell her. I wish I wasn't just this exotic creature to you.

She gets into the passenger side of the car and Roman's father, waving, sits behind the steering wheel.

"Nice to meet you!" Little calls, dashing forward to embrace me, then following her parents.

From the black of the night, white freckles meander downwards.

"Snow!" I cry, putting my hand out into the air. A million minute pieces.

Snow it is then, to cool the feet, to null and void those senses you still have. Snow it is that numbs your feet, that brings you to the earth again, holds you there, makes you kneel to its will. Snow it is that can melt a man, buoy him up, envelope him and make him coarse and cold. Snow does all these things because it is nature's possession. It possesses you as you possess it – it owns you as you own it.

But it is this possession, as with a lover, that can spell all kinds of small deaths.

*

The butterfly felt at ease with city now. She was in love with its infinite variety, its creation and recreation.

Resting on a park bench, the butterfly made out a shape near a rose bush. Its wings looked just like hers.

"What do you think you are doing?" the other her said.

"I wasn't sure if you were real or not," the butterfly replied. "We look so alike."

"Yes, I'm real", the other butterfly said. "And I don't like being stared at."

"What's your name?"

"Red Admiral," came the reply. He glanced around, as though someone might be listening to the conversation. "But, let me tell you – it's your name, too."

Sixteen

The ruptured thunder of firecrackers punctuates the morning as I look around the studio's infinity wall and lamps. An armoire and an armchair with stuffing trailing from its bottom are the main decorations; both have been covered in silver and wedged beneath the window ledge. Roman pushes a rack of white dresses towards the changing area that is divided from the main room by a sheer curtain, all of which have been loaned for free from fashion houses.

"Have a look," he says.

Checking them out, I have to concede that Amanda has a knack for getting what she wants. Just as I pick up a Valentino ball gown she whirls in, throwing a greeting at Roman.

"You're late," he says as she takes her coat off. She hugs him, then examines his face, murmuring softly in Mandarin. The intimacy of this gets hold. I feel excluded by their language, by the codes of behaviour that I can never hope to grasp.

Roman asks me to change into a sixties-style dress. Pulling it off the rack, I make my way to the changing area. I struggle to get it on; it's very nipped in at the waist. When I step out, Roman isn't there.

"He had to do an errand," Amanda says.

She powders my face and nose. When she goes for my hair, I take the brush from her.

"I'll do it."

"It's nice," Amanda says, her eyes shifting over my body, "A bit fat…" She grabs my right hip where the dress has rippled, giggling, "but no worry."

"I wasn't."

I try to pose in front of the infinity wall as Amanda starts with warm-up shots on a digital camera. She clicks her tongue, not happy with the set up. Fiddling with the dimmer switch, she nods at the armchair.

"Go there. Might be better. Kind of ruined."

I climb onto the chair and open the blind. On the courtyard outside, an artist breaks up painted canvases in an old oil canister. He pours lighter fluid on them and flicks out a match.

"You look at me now," she says, as the paintings explode into a fireball. "Think about something you love, or somebody. Or do you not love anybody?" The hint of a smile.

Snap, snap.

"I love somebody. Do you love somebody?"

From the corner of my eye, the fireball gains in height.

"I love somebody," she says. "At me, not outside."

Her smile puts my head in a vice. If she's goading me, it's working. I drop the pose and get up.

"Is it Roman?" My words rip through the thick air.

"Why does it have to be about that?" She lowers the camera.

"Students fall in love with their teachers all the time."

"You're such a child."

Amanda puts the camera on the shelf and leaves, slamming the door. Her footsteps trip-trap down stairs. I tug at the dress. The zip sticks. As I struggle, the door clicks open again. At least it's him.

"What are you doing?" he says, rushing over and undoing my zip.

"I'm not into team games, I thought I told you that."

"What?"

"This is not me," I shout, tugging my jeans back on. "I'm not this girl who hangs on a guy's arm at parties and wants to look pretty all the time. I don't need you. And I definitely don't need her."

I pull on my shoes and look for my handbag. Where is it? Manic, I search under the armchair while Roman looks on. I can't see it anywhere.

"You left your bag in the hotel, if that's what you're looking for. Do you want to get a bit of air?"

Outside, the fireball continues to burn.

94

"I guess."

The pavements are littered with red pieces of paper as we negotiate the wide paths of the district. The few pedestrians salute us with New Year's greetings as Roman peddles. Jiggling on the back of the bike, I wish for home. But where? There is no home, there's nothing like it. There's finding a place to pause and put your head, with the quiet hope that nobody will tell you to leave.

Roman steers us through what looks like a dead end but instead conceals another path to a park with a lake which glistens with the last fireworks being set off in the city centre. We ditch the bike. Roman tries to hold my hand as a Mozart concerto springs from an unknown source.

"I used to come here and read all the time when I was a kid," he says, leading me along a path.

We get to a tree, nude and defenceless against the sting of the winter. Padlocks dangle from red ribbons attached to its bough and branches. Roman pulls out a red gift bag from his backpack and gives it to me.

"I went to pick it up earlier when you were with Amanda. It was supposed to be your New Year's present. But now seems like a good time."

I open it. Inside is a brass padlock with an inscription written in Chinese and in English.

When two people are at one in their innermost hearts
They shatter even the strength of iron or of bronze
And when two people understand each other in their innermost hearts
Their words are sweet and strong like the fragrance of orchids.

He pulls a ribbon from his left breast pocket.

"I thought we could put it on together." Hooking a ribbon onto the padlock, he hangs it from a branch. "It's a cutesie type of tradition but I wanted to do it with you because I never did it with anyone."

"Did you choose the poem yourself?"

"I had help." Huh.

Reaching for my hand, he presses my fingers around the open lock. It clicks into place.

*

When we return to the studio, Roman resets the lights. I get changed, ignoring the misgivings resting in my gut as I immerse myself in white satin. Maybe it's infatuation, this desire to simultaneously conquer and be conquered. There's no other reason for such submission.

The door opens and closes from behind the changing room curtain. Amanda's voice. Roman and her have a flat-sounding chat. Silence. When I step out, she covers her face with her hair and picks up the make-up palette.

"About earlier," Roman starts, "She said she was trying to get you to react. It's my fault. I tell her that she has to bond with her subjects. But this time you insulted instead, eh, *Bao*?"

Amanda dabs at me with concealer; her face doesn't betray any reaction.

"*Bao*?"

"My nickname in Chinese," she says, stepping back to admire her handiwork.

Once a bottle of vodka has been opened, we all loosen up. Roman passes the camera to Amanda. She snaps much more tentatively than before.

"Think about what you hate," Amanda says.

Snap, snap.

"Think about what you love," Roman says.

Snap, snap.

Think about what you don't understand.

Snap, snap, snap.

*

"But if you're Red Admiral and I'm Red Admiral too, then it's going to complicate things if we start flying around together," the butterfly said.

"Pick another name, then," Red Admiral replied.

96

"I don't want a name. If you are having Red Admiral, then I will just be the butterfly."

"All right then," Red Admiral said, exasperated. "I'm going. Come with me, if you like."

"Do you know where we can find happiness?"

"I think so."

Side by side, they took flight.

Seventeen

The wall clock in the Japanese restaurant says two pm. I've been here since eight in the morning. For whatever reason a thread of guilt creeps up on me. But a writer has to write. Right?

The setup for the celebrations continues full-speed beneath the Bell Tower as I make my way back to the hotel. A stage and speaker system have been set up since last night. Anticipation mingles with uncertainty: the essence of drama.

When I reach our street, fully-grown men are exploding things. Fireworks are let off from inside the complexes, several of them travelling too close to the roofs of the nearby buildings. The red roofs curl upwards to the heavens, smiling on in the face of the assault.

A cart holder pitched at the hotel entrance sells fish-shaped firecrackers to children who barely rise above the knee, then ushers them a few yards away from the rest of his wares. The resulting machine-gun fire follows me up the steps.

"Miss, Miss!" the bellhop calls in an English accent, bounding outside to get the door with the sort of gusto that's adopted if there's the hope of a tip. "Allow me!"

"*Xiexie*," I reply, stepping into the lobby where the lad who was serving yesterday has since been replaced by a rotund middle-aged woman immersed in a crossword puzzle.

"Your Chinese is very good!" the bellhop comments, pressing the bell for the lift. I hand him twenty *kuai*.

"*Xin nian kuai le!*" he says.

Singing emanates from the shower when I get back to our room. Straightening things out, I plop down on the bed. Roman comes out of the bathroom towelling himself off. With a burp, he opens his bag and rootles through his clothes.

"Did you sleep well?" I ask him. He burps again, selecting trousers and a t-shirt. Did he hear?

"Did you sleep well?" Nothing. "What's the matter?"

"I didn't know where you were," he says, sitting on the bed and administering a sock to his left foot.

"I was writing. I got you lunch!" I hold out the now unappetising-looking pancake I purchased on the way back.

"Why can't you get a cell phone like a normal person? I have a meeting about the new exhibition." He jumps up and splashes on aftershave. "We'll have dinner with my parents tonight. I'll get you back here at five."

"Will Amanda be joining us?" I ask, unable keep the note of cattiness from my voice. Ignoring me, he lets himself out. I count to thirty and make for the stairs.

In the street, the darkness is already coming. I walk for a long time, attempting to reconcile doubts with a sense of obligation. Perhaps it was too soon. Perhaps we didn't know each other well enough. Perhaps, perhaps, perhaps.

At the Muslim Quarter, I get lost in the labyrinth of a walkthrough shopping mall. Patterned silks float from the ceilings; Russian dolls and knick-knacks dot table tops. The shops are filled with delicacies; fruit sellers flog gluts of tangerines as though they're going out of fashion. At the other end of the maze, I notice a phonebooth with amusement. A novelty now. I'll take it as an intervention from the universe. Who should I call? I only know two numbers off by heart.

I fumble in my pocket for change, dial. Several rings before I get an answer.

"Hello?" Rose says, grandly. Dance music is pumping in the background. Immediate comfort. Rose and the never-ending Shanghai carousal are still out there.

"It's me. Where are you?"

"Happy New Year! I don't know, to be honest. Let me ask..." She shouts to someone in the background who yells back. "That was Pierre. He doesn't know either. Hang on, I'm going outside. I think it's Fuzhou Road. The fireworks are on soon! It's been crazy all day. I haven't stopped for almost sixty hours. Why the hell aren't you here?"

"I'm still in Xi'an. It's not going very well."

A squealing noise on the other end mixes with laughter.

"Hold up!" she says. The noise subsides.

"I'm on the balcony," she says. "Jesus, this is beautiful. You'll be okay, it's just a holiday. Now listen, I've got to tell you something important. I tried to get hold of you. I left you messages on Roman's phone."

"He never said anything."

"We got evicted last week. Not just us, the whole *longtang*. I just came back one day and there was an official form waiting for us. Even people who lived there for twenty years got the same deal. Leaving was quite fun, actually. I had beers with the neighbours in the lane while we were all surrounded by suitcases. They kept asking to take photos with me. I'm crashing with Veronica now. I've got all of your stuff. Well, the one bag of things. And your notebooks."

"Why didn't Roman pass the messages on?"

Rose doesn't have an answer. Outside, coils of people push past metal barriers on their way to the Bell Tower where the light show is starting in couple of hours.

"What else have you been doing with yourself?" I ask, leaning heavily against the side of the booth.

"I had a gig for a commercial yesterday. Had to play a mermaid again. It's a bit of a fad."

"I miss you."

"I miss you, too, honey. And don't take any shit from Roman."

"I didn't realise you didn't like him."

"I don't *not* like him," she says, as diplomatic an utterance as is possible for her to utter. "But I don't *like* like him. He's a Little Emperor. Any rich kid can hold a camera, live on Daddy's money and make out that he's a hotshot. Is his cock even very big?"

"I don't want to talk about his cock if it's all the same to you."

"Okay, fine," she says. "When are you coming back?"

"I could leave now. What would you do?"

"You've got your ticket, haven't you? Just make nice till you get back, then ditch him. It's only a week."

"Isn't that a bit morally questionable?"

"Is it morally questionable of him to be a douchebag?"

I let her have it.

Hanging up the phone, strategy after strategy leads my imagination on a merry dance. I follow the path to the East Road. A crowd forms beside the cordoned-off area as a Dragon Dance thunders along at the front of a procession with drummers playing accompaniment. Rejuvenated by the sight of it, I join the fray, clapping along. The leader of the dance holds the dragonhead close to a kid standing in front of me. The kid squeals with pleasure; the rest of us join in. The dancers continue on their gold and red journey.

*

"Where are we?" the butterfly asked Red Admiral, *when she realised that she could no longer hear the din of any oncoming traffic.*

"We're going to the countryside," Red Admiral replied. *"If you want to go back, feel free."*

The butterfly paused in the air. She had just started to get to know the city, but her instinct told her to follow Red Admiral. He might know where to find happiness, after all.

"I'll stay with you," the butterfly said.

They slipped through the dark. The urban shapes dimmed into memory.

Eighteen

Over twenty members of Roman's extended family mill around the courtyard of the *siheyuan*, a quadrangle of living quarters he grew up in. The symmetry of the construction is draped with New Year's lanterns hanging from balustrades. Additions to the same suspects from the restaurant include Roman's grandparents on both sides, an uncle from his mother's side and another cousin in his twenties, Walter.

A good deal of fuss is made over our arrival by the older members of the family. Roman's grandmother pinches his cheeks and holds out red envelopes to both of us.

"She doesn't speak any English," Roman tells me. I shake her hand and we smile at each other, shyly. She gives me the envelope.

"You have to take it," Roman, squeezing my elbow when I hesitate.

"*Xiexie*," I say, making an attempt at a bow just as Little bounds over and embraces me from behind. Roman and his grandmother look on, chatting.

"I want to show you my room!" Little says. Taking me by the hand, she leads me into the tallest building. It doesn't seem as though I have a choice in the matter.

"This is the main house. We live here, too! My father wasn't so well in the head for a while, so Roman's family say they will take care of us. My father thought he was going crazy, but he had a tumour. Now he is okay."

When we reach the second floor, Little darts inside the door closest to the landing. "Here we are!"

Decorated in red and dominated by a four-poster bed, it is more sexpot boudoir than teenage wasteland. This must be intentional; Little definitely comes off as a forward-thinker. Lines of DVDs and fashion books take up an entire wall. A notebook lies by the bed, open on a sketch of a woman in a tailored suit holding an umbrella.

"These are my designs!" She thrusts the notebook at me. Even I can tell she has a talent. "It's the only thing I can do well. I hate maths. But I will do it so that I can start my fashion label." She puts the designs into a drawer and we head out into the hallway where the light is falling for what will be the last time this lunar year.

"I take you up the elevator!" she says, leading me to the black doors.

"I thought we were at the top."

"You have to see Roman's room."

Curiosity overcomes. "Sure."

In contrast to the traditional style of the rest of the house, Roman's self-contained apartment is coolly modern in style and looks over Xi'an, where night dyes the city ready for play. Piles of books and unused equipment are abandoned in the corner.

"I come up here when nobody else is home. I'm not supposed to, but Roman is never around and I like the peacefulness. My father," she drops her voice to a more discrete volume although no-one will hear, a socialite in the making, "thinks Roman is spoilt. He always get what he want. He always making his film. But he never stick to anything."

"Oh?"

"He want to go study in America, he go to America. He want to go to Europe, he go to Europe. But my father always say he never finish anything, and he never happy with anything he do. So he gets more."

"I see." It might be wise to steer clear of this line of conversation, not least because I am starting to agree with the sentiments expressed. A gust of wind hustles through the room.

"Why are all the windows open?"

"To let go of the old year," Little says.

As she wanders back to the lift, I have to wonder whether Roman's dissatisfaction with everything comes from having the world so freely offered to him in the first place.

Vases of plum blossoms and lilies dot the table in the dining room. Dishes of gingko, bean curd, scallion and vermicelli are sandwiched between bowls of oranges and persimmons. Servants bring in noodles, fat whole chickens steamed with bok choy and vats of fish in chilli and garlic.

I am sat next to Walter, who talks at length about his impending marriage to Liu who couldn't be at the dinner this evening because her family lives in Hong Kong. As I listen, the warmth of celebration distracts me from deeper thoughts.

By five to midnight, traditional Chinese opera music belts from the speakers in the courtyard. Roman's Dad, who has the same curly hair and willful temperament as his son, places a box of firecrackers, sparklers and other explosives on a trussed table. We dive for them as midnight looms.

"*Xin nian kuai le!*" We yell as the clock slips past twelve.

Everyone is a blur of embraces. Rockets hit the sky, blasting titter tatters of noise at the people on earth. To New Year, to new Prosperity.

*

At dawn, Roman and me slip up to his studio to make love overlooking the city. He pushes me against the wall, his hand moving up my skirt. I'm not there; I feel wary of him now. I just want it to be over.

"What's wrong?" he says.

"Nothing." I can't tell him, it would be even worse. No. The self-mutilation of passive aggressive behaviour is the answer. "I don't feel like it."

"You know how ungrateful you are," he says, as I pull away and take my clothes off.

"Ungrateful?" I can't help but let out a laugh.

"Yeah. Think about all I've done for you. The portraits, the exhibitions."

I don't care. Do I?

"Of course. I'm just a girl. And you're the prince."

"I didn't mean it like that," he says, softly. I get into bed.

"Goodnight, dear prince," I reply, without a trace of sarcasm.

Tired from his assertions of himself, I pass out.

*

The butterfly found it difficult to keep up with Red Admiral, whose wings were larger than her own. Occasionally Red Admiral paused to check that she was still there, but otherwise he kept to one distinct path. As they moved through the forest, she wondered if she would lose him in the night.

"I mustn't stop," the butterfly thought, as they flew and flew.

Nineteen

Behind the desk where hosts hover with guest lists, a portrait of a woman is emblazoned with the title *Cerebral*. Me, Roman and his other, other half are ushered past and down the staircase by the Managing Director of the gallery, a school friend of Roman's whose English name is Chad.

"We've had calls about the show all day," Chad says, marching ahead of us in a perfectly cut suit. "The stuff you made was superb. And you," he turns to me, all charm and management, "are a natural."

I mutter a thank you, unable to shake the sense of feeling over-exposed. As we make our way through the maze of tunnels, I scan the other pictures on display. The styles vary from the surreal to the romantic.

When we reach the main auditorium, over a hundred people are already circulating with canapés and champagne. I survey the scene: art critics mixed with hipsters and the odd proud family member.

Amanda's photos are displayed on one wall; mostly blown-out black and white prints of subjects wearing white. They have been taken either in fields or on beaches, apart from the shot of me. A suited man in his thirties taps me on the shoulder and holds out his hand. The man introduces himself as Sid.

"You're different in the flesh. Care to join me? I'm here to do a review."

"I'm with my..." I trail off. There he is, talking intensely with Amanda. Well, Sid's company will beat flying solo.

Two hours and at least five more glasses of champagne later, I'm on top of the world again and believe I have made a new friend for life in Sid, who is a journalist for a Chinese arts magazine called *Hoof*. He's from Beijing and is in Xi'an on business. As we hover by the bar, he divulges his honest opinion of the works on display.

"It's like – cerebral. We get it. Cerebral people dress in white and float around. That's what being cerebral is. Anything else to add?"

I definitely like Sid.

"Do you want another drink?" he says.

Over Sid's shoulder, I scout Roman talking to a woman in her fifties with the grounded air of a critic. Amanda is hanging by his right hand side, no doubt substantiating his every statement with an obscure intellectual reference. As I watch them, distrust mixes with desire. It's at once heady and toxic.

"Yes I would."

*

After midnight, Sid leaves for his hotel. I end up in the bathroom where more coke appears in front of me. It quickly comes off the ceramic tile and into my nose. I wonder about my nose sometimes. Whether it will fall off. Then I could be the nose-less woman and everybody would know what a freak I really am.

Roman comes in as I am washing my hands. He pulls my face towards him, peering up my nostrils.

"You doing that again?"

"What does it matter?" I extricate myself.

"You're embarrassing me. Can't you save it for later?"

"Face, is it?" I put lipstick on.

"Don't pretend to understand," Roman says, walking out.

When I return to the party, neither he nor Amanda is there.

Apropos of everything, I make my way back through the tunnels.

*

When I let myself into the hotel room, the sound of piano playing wafts from a nearby apartment block. The warm harmonies emphasise the discord. The earlier parts of the evening revisit; mind games I can't remember the specifics of now, except that they have got me to this point. Not solitude, of which I am very fond. Loneliness, its unkind relative.

There is more oxygen by the window. Four floors below, in a living room opposite, the piano player's back bounces to his tune. As the music becomes more sensual, the notes longer and more languid, the player hunches closer to the keys.

Maybe Roman is simply another dilettante. Out of interests, loves, friendships, pleasures, places. A shifting soul. I have projected onto him. I could be wrong, but projection means living forward. That's what I thought I was doing. But what do I know? Only that the deepest parts of the night are the most inspiring. I pick up my notebook.

*

The high is still there when I lie awake at five am and two sets of footsteps enter the room. I swallow any questions. I am a fool. A fool in love; the most foolish sort of fool.

I pretend to be asleep until a snapping sound whips me up in fright. Roman is taking photographs of Amanda lounging on the sofa. On the table in front of them is an open bottle of vodka and some drugs or other. All I can think is how correct they are as a pair, the answer to a mathematical equation.

"Baby, I thought you'd left me." Roman lifts the camera to his right eye again and refocuses the lens on me. He snaps again.

Amanda breaks open a baggie of pills. Ecstasy. She smiles at me and holds the bag out. Well, I'm not beating them. Hesitating, I pop one in my mouth and swallow it with vodka.

"I want to take more photos of you," he says, moving over to me. "Amanda does, too."

"I'm not well," she says, her eyes suggesting she's cruising well above planet earth. "You're not well, either."

"You're both women who don't love anything," Roman says, running his hand through my hair. "Women who aren't even human."

She puts the stereo on and brings the vodka over to us on the bed.

Sitting on Roman's knee, she starts to stroke the inside of his thigh. A thigh I thought was mine. Their collective power paralyses me. Worse, I'm starting to fear it.

"She's sick," Roman says, showing me the picture on the LCD screen. "She exists for herself and in herself. She gets eaten. Eaten by herself."

The picture is of my eye. Extreme close-up. Green and blue strands of colour. Red veins on the off-white of the ball.

"A misanthrope?" I ask, as Amanda's fingers grow more exploratory. I curl my legs away from them.

Without answering, Roman lies back on the bed. Lyrics of a song I don't recognise sweep insidiously through the room. Our limbs are so close they are almost unified.

He starts to kiss me on the neck, moving to my nipples. I feel love again: the chemical kind. Eyes and body parts in fragments. Hers, his, my own. Their legs face each other. I am briefly conscious only of the feral rhythm and bass line. Roman stops kissing my body and moves back up to my face.

"Take off your dress," he tells Amanda. The dress, pure white, appears on the floor from over her head. They kiss. I am never enough. The room is smothering.

"You're a bomb, a red bomb," Amanda leans forwards, kissing me on the mouth. Her breasts press against my rib cage. I kiss her back. As we continue I feel more pleasure. I feel it. Don't I?

"Why are you so shy, baby?" Roman says.

I'm not shy. I'm not that girl. You don't know me at all.

"Why don't you let her touch you? Her skin is so soft." Brainlessly, I watch as her hand slides over my breasts, belly, pussy. His camera snaps, snaps. I can do this.

I put my hand on her tit. Warm and firm. As I massage the nipple, the camera in Roman's hand makes its pictures. He moves between us slowly while we kiss, not really with us but acting out a scene in his mind. She pulls at my t-shirt; it comes off too. Seamless. Smooth.

Roman puts the camera down on the nightstand. He starts to kiss Amanda's feet, legs, inside her thighs. Moving up her body, he bites her on the arse. She moans; pleasure and pain. The ecstasy drifts through me. I am wet. I am in it.

I lean forward and kiss him. He goes from her to me. His tongue in my mouth. He tastes of her. His hand strokes between my legs, faster and faster. With the other he pushes my head back to her. I fight the urge to laugh, but it comes out. Desperation? I don't know. My senses aren't working properly; the room is doing a lurching dance.

"Ruby," Amanda says, kissing me on the belly and pulling off my knickers. "Why are you so shy?"

"You'll never understand anything, do you know that?" Roman leans back on his haunches. His eyes are flattened by the alcohol. Fish eye.

"I understand. I understand." I'm not sure if it's my voice saying these words, or the voice that he has given me through this puppetry. Is it because I'm scared of losing him? Dumb, I lean in.

The three of us end up on the floor. I can feel Roman's mouth on my belly, then on her, then her face, my face, her tits, mine. I stroke his hair. At once out of it and in it, I'm wet again. His cock goes in. Everything else continues centred on this action, on its tormenting sweetness.

*

When insomnia kicks in, I am drawn to thoughts of whether there is a point in a man looking at himself in running water rather than still water. When the water should be still; whether the water will ever be still at all. Whether or not if you were to stop, if you were to think really deeply about what you do every day and the pockets of time that you fill doing the things you do; if you were to add it all up, or to write it down, if you were to do those things, what the result would be? I guess you'd be as scared as I have been for a long time now. You'd be as fucked as god. And, ultimately, you'd probably want to escape.

*

110

As morning broke, the flowers extended their petals and the trees held out their branches, welcoming the butterfly home. But still, she found herself longing for the city. She missed the vitality of the people in it. She missed their noise and smell. The country, by comparison, was soundless. Still, at least Red Admiral was there. If she could stay with him, then maybe things would work out for the best.

Twenty

As I make my way down Mount Hua, the shape of the plantations reminds me of the Highlands. I catch my breath. The sun dips low, casting fingers onto the path behind me and stretching up to the ten or so lodges nestled in the enclaves. Perhaps this is the top of the world. Simplicity. Satisfaction. An hour outside of Xi'an but it might as well be in a different country.

It was a relief to leave them this morning. To close the door and shut off what I know isn't right but have been unable to extricate myself from. For a while, though, I can do what I've proven to have one talent at: running away.

I continue to trip downwards, the wind gusting up and between my legs. This dress. Rose gave it me. The yellow sings. Too yellow for her, she said. Branches break from behind. A man dressed in a windbreaker and hiking shoes catches up with me.

"Aren't you cold?" He means my thin coat.

"I am," I reply, laughing. "I'm always cold."

"I'm the lodge owner, my name is Wang. The workers saw you arriving. One of them came up to me and told me there was a witch on the mountain. He'd never seen red hair before."

Wang walks slowly and reaches a hand out to balance me as we walk off the main pathway and through a glade that I would probably not have noticed, although previous footsteps have treaded a trail through it. The glade leads onto chickens scratching in a courtyard next to a log cabin. A few streaks of light trickle from within the cabin, along with the smell of cooking.

"How did you end up here?" I ask, as we skirt around the chickens. Disturbed, they strut to their coop.

"I was a banker. I lived in Beijing for most of my life," he says. "I worked so hard. Cities make you measure everything in terms of your own success. They're the most populated places on earth but at the same time the most lonely. A few years ago, I took my savings and built this place. Here, none of that matters. I wouldn't go back."

He pushes the cabin door ajar. Inside, an elderly woman works at the stove in a kitchen. The flame glistens blue, casting a reflection on the collection of bowls at the side containing garlic powder, onion and chilli. Her hands are precise as she chops mushrooms, noodles and greens. She adds them to the smoking wok without noticing us.

"Why don't you take a rest?" Wang says. "The *ayi* is in there. I have to go back to see my wife for lunch."

"Thank you."

He descends some steps hidden by foliage on the other side of the courtyard. The *ayi* turns the gas on the ring down and puts a cover over the top of the pan, moving to a storeroom. She still doesn't see me. Not wanting to disturb her, I follow Wang's path.

*

As I climb down the mountain, I have the awake-dream of unity. Abundance. Fields. Renewal. Breaking away from the path, I walk through the lined fields of rapeseed. The dress is torn at the bottom. It keeps catching on the tips of the bare branches. I have never felt so thirsty. I have never wanted to drink as badly as I do now. I can't see water. I keep moving. There must be water. At the end, there will be water.

*

The room is unlocked although Roman and Amanda aren't there. The light is off. The night lives in shadows, too.

I put the light on. The stuff I left on the desk has been moved.

A bird hops about on the ledge. It's a brownish thing, save for one white spot on its lower back. This is the first bird I have encountered the whole time I have been living in China, aside from the ones sold in cages at the markets. Maybe I am seeing things; confusing the real with the imagined again.

I need to find food for the bird. In this moment, it is the most important thing that I can do. I look through the plastic supermarket bags on the counter top and find a baguette end, discarded from a few days ago. I break it up and put it on a side plate.

The door opens and closes. Roman. He is alone. I open the window and put the plate on the ledge beside the bird.

"Hey baby," Roman says, softly, kissing my shoulder. I can't reciprocate.

I cannot be this girl. I cannot.

"What are you doing?"

"Feeding a bird." The bird takes a fragment of the bread and nibbles it, shifting its head back and forth.

"You take everything so serious." He giggles, nervousness combined with amusement. I don't feel safe. But I still want him to love me, more than he loves her. The bird vanishes.

"What's wrong with you?" Roman says, putting his hands on my shoulders. "Don't you think, if you expose yourself to the things that might hurt you, you become strong? Now you're weak."

"Nihilistic bullshit is not love."

"If you were going to go, you would have left already. But you haven't. You wanted me to teach you a lesson, didn't you?"

I wanted a guide, I realise, more than a lover. "Maybe," I reply.

"You love this," he says.

"I don't." I don't.

The sheets have sex stains on them. Opening the wardrobe to find fresh ones, I notice Amanda's shoes next to Roman's boots. They look the size a child would wear.

I eventually locate sheets in the drawer underneath the bed. As I strip the old ones off, Roman's phone rings which leads to a long conversation in Chinese. I finish making the bed. A knock at the door. Guess who.

*

114

Sleeping time, but not for me. Roman snores in the middle of the bed. Amanda is on the furthest side. I'm the peeping tom now. There is nothing left to think about.

I go to the wardrobe. As I pull my bag out, the noise disturbs Amanda but she doesn't wake up. I crush my clothes into it and let myself out as quietly as I can.

Outside, I find myself running down the street. Energy borne from hurt. I run and I run until I can't breathe any more.

*

The straight pavements littered with crêpe paper have long since faded into ring roads and industrial estates, solely distinguished by the different pharmaceutical company headquarters. The further I walk, the more these increase in width and austerity, space and severity.

I should have left a note. A note saying what, though?

Toll signs flicker about a kilometre away. I continue in their direction until I reach the metal barriers. I slip through, unnoticed. I'm struck by how post apocalyptic it feels, although perhaps that's just pathetic fallacy rearing its ugly head.

In the layby, a four-by-four is parked with its emergency lights on but nobody inside. About five-hundred metres further down is a bus next to a stop. The driver lurks beside the hood, smoking and talking into his mobile phone.

"Shanghai?" I ask.

He snaps his phone shut and holds up two fingers.

"*Liang bai*," he says. I pull out a couple of red notes. In exchange, he passes me a green ticket stump.

"Leave one hour. No late," he says, with effort.

"*Xin nian kuai le*," I reply, clambering onto the bus. Collapsing onto the nearest seat, I don't even have enough energy to cry.

*

In the centre of the forest, the butterfly lost Red Admiral. Straining to

115

see him again, she perched beside a sunflower and noticed the group of ladybirds. It was better to talk to them than nobody at all.

"Hello!" she called out to the leader of the group.

"Hi!" the leader of the ladybirds called back. "Do I know you?"

"We met a while ago," the butterfly said. "Don't you remember me?"

The leader of the ladybirds inspected the butterfly.

"Oh, of course!" the leader of the ladybirds said. "Where have you been?"

"I went to the city," the butterfly said.

Twenty-one

The outlook from the penthouse skims over downtown where the warm glow cast by the towers of the financial district and the nearby hospital creates calm. Rose's new room is the size of our old flat, complete with en-suite bathroom and walk-in wardrobe. Art Nouveau paintings of semi-naked men and women score the walls.

"This is it," Rose says.

This is the *new* it.

"Jesus!" I flip through her collection of clothes. It has tripled in size since I left. My possessions from the flat at Chongqing lie at the bottom of her bed.

I trail my hand on the wrought iron banister as we make our way downstairs. Photographs line the path, on most walls and available surfaces. All are of Veronica with glamorous people in casinos, clubs, theatres and cinemas. She doesn't seem to operate in daylight.

When we reach the living room, Rose pops the cork on a bottle of champagne.

"To arriving! And to your new-found freedom!"

The swig I take goes directly from my head to the tips of my toes.

"Should I have left a note?" I ask her for the hundredth time.

"What could you have said?"

"Something?" Maybe something is better than nothing.

"Let me show you the balcony!" Rose says, bored by my seriousness and still fluttering with the thrill of her new life.

Outside, I lean over the railing to test how far I can see. Almost to Pudong. Everything twinkles from up here. It fits Rose, or the new version of herself she will be incubating in this particular environment.

At least two bottles are consumed and several hours seep past as we talk about the shows that Rose has attended in my absence, the openings that have been thrown, the tittle-tattle of who did what to whom, the drugs consumed, the men avoided and slept with, the potential conquests that didn't work out. Ashok didn't call her over the New Year's holiday.

"I need to find a way to plot my revenge." Rose takes revenge fairly seriously. "But then, Rodrigo wants to fly me to Thailand on his private jet on Monday."

"How many people can say that they have Italian men with cognitive capacities intact and their own plane offering to take them to Thailand on a whim?"

"It's not as straightforward as that," she says.

"Why?" I ask her. "Go for it!"

Rose is elsewhere now. The silhouette of her face curves on the side of the building as she sips the last of her champagne. The subject is closed.

"Come on," she says, rising from the recliner. "Let's get ready."

*

At *Straw Dogs*, the bouncer who doesn't acknowledge anyone again fails to crack a smile despite the spirit of the New Year. Michelle greets us by the coat check and tells us that we have special guests to entertain tonight. For once, *Straw Dogs* is playing host to foreigners who are here – gasp – voluntarily.

"I put it to you," Michelle says, her new twang suggesting she may have indulged in a few too many American courtroom television dramas recently, "to make sure that the group of male dancers from Las Vegas has the best time possible."

This is a significant turn-up for the yet-to-be-completed book.

"We'll do it!" Rose says, as though a commando about to attempt her first attack on land. Patting her hair, she leads the dual charge towards the group of dancers: a collective of sinew and dark hair. They have been seated at a table in the far corner that has been cordoned off with red rope. A sign saying *IP AREA* is perched beside the rope.

As we make our way over, Rose keeps her head high, clocking the dancing boys individually. In an effort not to think about things I shouldn't, I hover next to Jonathan, who has a bone structure to die for and hips smaller than mine. He barely pauses to ask my name before launching into a story about holidays he takes in Vancouver every year with the others. His description of shirtless fly-fishing resembles a pubescent sexual fantasy.

"When you're lost on a boat in the river it's so quiet out that you can hear your pulse," Jonathan drawls, staring into my eyes. "Let me show you our routine for the new show, it's killer."

He is not my type but there's confusion all around. Besides, it's the jangling of the ten thousand things that keep the fire burning; the chaos that keeps you warm at night. As Jonathan shimmies onto the floor, Ashok turns up on my right hand side, watching as Rose struts her stuff with Jimmy or Jamie.

"She's moved on quick," Ashok comments as Rose and Jimmy or Jamie go at it, groin to groin. I am again struck by how minutely his face changes when he's talking: a human plaster mould. Dejected, he helps himself to the jug of vodka and real orange juice placed on the low table.

"Rose is so insensitive. I'm very sensitive, you know," Ashok says. "I'm an actor."

Ashok downs the vodka concoction and makes his way back to the other male models. Poor Ashok. While I may lament my unfortunate end with Roman, love twixt actors must be even more complicated than other forms of love, what with the additional ego problems and ultra-sensitivity already involved. When the song gets to the chorus, Jonathan contorts his body in expert poses. I give him a round of applause.

As Jonathan makes his way back to the IP area, a very drunk local girl accosts him.

"I think I love you!" she yells, the force of her words booming over the mega mix. Just as tears are starting to trickle down her face, the bouncer strong-arms the girl towards the front entrance. A couple of sheepish kids, presumably her friends, follow the wails.

"What the hell just happened?" Jonathan asks me.

"This is China." I reply.

"This is China?"

I can't even explain any more.

*

After closing, it doesn't take long to get to the dancers' hotel, which is overrun with staff wearing over-the-top security headsets as though under imminent terrorist threat. The other brothers, save the Jimmy or Jamie that Rose has gone off with for the night, have failed to score and retire to bed. Jonathan and I go for a nightcap. As we wait the twenty floors worth of distance in the lift, Jonathan stares at me.

In the bar, there are no other guests. Jonathan orders two bourbons. The sun is starting to rise. I get the glorious echoing feeling that comes with having stayed up all night wasting your time, but not wasting it at all. Jonathan slides closer.

"Have I told you about Vancouver?" Before I can say anything, he continues. "When you're lost on a boat in the river it's so quiet out that you can hear..."

"Your pulse?"

I wonder how many thousands of girls he must have used that one on over the years.

"Wow, it's like you were there with me."

He leans in for the kill. His lips are within mauling distance. But still, a playboy with a bad memory is probably not the best way to get over an injured heart.

"I'm sorry," I mutter.

Without waiting for his response, I skip over to the lift and out into the morning. I don't have enough money left from tonight's pay to get a taxi, having purchased two bottles of champagne and enough coke to alleviate the Roman-grief.

Trying to negotiate the alien turf of the northern Bund on foot, I realise I have no idea where I am. Empty beer bottles lie abandoned from a heavy night. Nobody's home. This isn't like you, Shanghai.

At the *Kedi*, I buy a bottle of wine. The counter boy, as though by telepathy, hands me a paper cup. His smile suggests life might get better.

Pity from the dude working the graveyard shift in a convenience shop: arguably the lowest of lows.

Paper cup and wine in hand, I make my way to the Bund. The Toshiba skyscraper is switched on and the television screens on the side blink to life. An advertisement. A woman feeding her children dumplings. The dumplings have green insides; the stuffing spills out onto the plate. The children smile.

There must be a fuckup because, once it draws to a close, the advert repeats itself again. The mother brings the dumplings out, and the children want to eat them. The green spills out. There it goes again. The same advert with the same smiles. Over and over.

The outline of docked cruise liners breaks the horizon. I inevitably find my thoughts straying to Roman.

Love: the biggest con going. Addendum: excluding Scientology.

A scraping noise from my left gives way to an old man peddling a wagon attached to his bicycle. On the back of the wagon is a glass case filled with plums coated in white sugar. The old man tips his cap as he sees me and slows to a halt.

"You're up early," he says in Mandarin. I think that's what he says.

"Where are you going?" I ask him in Mandarin.

The old man smiles at my efforts at Chinese and points to the Bund. I hold out the bottle of wine. He shakes his hand for a no. Dismounting the bicycle, he opens the case. After a moment of scrutiny, he selects three plums and puts them in a bag.

I make to pay for them with the change from the wine, but he shakes his hand again.

"Eat," he says, popping one in his mouth and pointing to the remaining fruit. *"You're too thin."*

A bite: the sugar scratches the inside of my mouth. I push my remaining *kuai* into his hands. He protests but takes the money and then bundles a few more into the bag for good measure. Closing the case, he starts peddling in the direction of the area where the tourists will gather later.

Random acts of kindness are the most cheering sort. Past the concession buildings and banks, I reach the sign for the ferry. Through the turnstiles and at the far end of the waiting room, the screens blare with fluorescent timetables indicating that there is one minute to wait.

The other person in the waiting room is a man in a suit on his way to work. The hostess, dressed in an aquamarine minidress, hollers an instruction and the suited man gathers his briefcase. I follow him out onto the boat, taking a seat by the window.

The engine gives a thud and chugs us towards Pudong. No birds in the sky. Instead, the standard foggy hue.

The horizon grows as we move through the water.

Stepping off at the other side, I follow the suited man to the exit. On the street, I manage to get both Puxi and Pudong in my eye-line. As I take in at the aspirations clashing with history, I realise what it is that I want. To make one thing that belongs to me. With the dregs of the red wine in my cup, I salute the city.

*

I wake up to a guard poking me on the shoulder. I jerk up; where the hell am I? I look around. I'm in a park. In Pudong. The guard takes out a packet of cigarettes and offers me one. I shake my head. He takes a long drink from his flask, sizing me up.

As I try to remember the events that have lead to waking up on a park bench, the guard picks up his walkie-talkie and speaks into it. The length of the guard's cigarette later, a policeman parks his car beside us and gets out, dusting his coat.

"You have an ID?" the policeman asks, in fairly smooth English. He's not much older than me.

The sun, ignoring the potential gravity of the situation, sticks its head out through the smog. I open my handbag and pull out my passport. The policeman flicks through the empty pages until he finds the visa. The guard's strained expression is unsettling; nausea hits.

"You are a tourist, yes?" The policeman asks, intently.

"Yes."

"You not working here?"

"No." Now is as good a time for fabrication as any.

"What is name of your hotel?"

"Hotel..." Come on brain. "...Nowhere."

It's not technically a lie.

"Where is Hotel Nowhere?"

I wave a hand in the direction of Puxi, my heartbeat tripping over itself. The policeman and the guard then talk for over half-an-hour, their speech peppered with mentions of Hotel Nowhere. Not for the first time, I'm glad I don't understand what is being said.

"You should go with him," the policeman says, pointing to the guard. "It's dangerous to be here this early in the morning."

The subway is located about five hundred metres further up the park and close to a shopping complex. I perch on the back end of the guard's bicycle as he peddles in its direction.

When we reach the sign, I tell the guard to stop and dismount before he can tell me not to. Intense claustrophobia and anxiety bury into my back and shoulders. As I continue down the escalator to the station, my chest tightens and my breath comes in gulps.

"*Laowai!*" A sniggering voice drifts from my right.

Leaning heavily on the moving handrail of the escalator, my heart flutters faster and faster at the necks craning, the mouths moving in whispers, the stares.

*

"Why did you come back?" the leader of the ladybirds said. "If I could fly all the way there, I would never come back."

"I followed Red Admiral," the butterfly said. "But I lost him."

"Silly. You should have stayed there."

"I might find him again," the butterfly replied.

"The forest is huge," the leader of the ladybirds said. "Good luck!"

The ladybirds walked away from the sunflower, leaving the butterfly behind.

"Goodbye!" the butterfly called after them. As she turned towards the tip of the sunflower, she felt more alone than ever.

Twenty-two

From afar, I have a sudden revelation about what Ashok's dancing reminds me of: a conveyor belt in a factory. That robotic monotony that must surely go along with the filling of ice-cream containers, the creation of lava lamps, or any other mass-produced plastic man dolls out there.

Three beats and he will thrust the right leg out. There we go. Another three beats and the left leg will go out. There we go. The finale of this move is brief gyration of the hips, which adds another four beats. There we go. And back to the right leg. Thrust. As I'm watching, Michelle taps me on the right shoulder.

"Ruby, I need to speak to you both," she says, beckoning Rose.

The Management Office is warmer than the rest of the bar. The boss' cousin is still playing solitaire on the computer and smoking weed. He might even be wearing the same clothes as the last time I saw him.

Michelle tells us to take a seat. Well, if she sacks us at least it will be a funny story. Losing possibly the easiest and most inconsequential job in the world.

Mantra: nothing bad ever happens to a writer.

"We're closing *Straw Dogs*," Michelle says. "They upped the rent. I've got another job at *Evil*." She picks up two envelopes lying beside her computer and hands them to us. "Last payment. We'll close tonight."

"So soon?" Rose says.

"It's Shanghai. Things change quickly. There's a bonus in there, too. For being good sports."

There isn't anything left to discuss. When we reach the hall, Rose opens her envelope. "Some bonus," she says sarcastically, examining at the contents.

"Fuck," is all I can say. It's only a few hundred *kuai*. Perhaps this isn't funny and is, in fact, dire.

Pulling up our stools at the bar, we commiserate over the usual tepid drinks.

"I should probably stick to acting anyway," Rose says, pocketing the envelope and fidgeting with matches on the counter in front of her. "Clouds and silver linings. I don't want to damage my credibility."

"I wonder about my credibility," I reply. "Mainly, whether or not I have any to damage."

Long past closing time, DJ Seven departs to the *Exit* sign with one of the dancers with complicated hair for what will be his final surreptitious shag. I tear up.

Noticing the decks are unmanned, Rose jumps on and selects an electronica track. I salute her from dancefloor. Evidently drunk with power as well as alcohol, she starts to mess with the levels. When the track finishes silence descends. DJ Seven emerges from the *Exit* to resume his position, followed by the tousled dancer, her hair less complicated now. Rose beats a retreat.

The music returns to the mash-up they play every night. I love it now. Probably because I know it's the last time I'll have to dance to it.

When the track reaches the now infamous trance version of *Happy Birthday*, Michelle brings over a bottle of prosecco. Popping the cork, she draws the contingent of male models and us together on the dance floor.

"To *Straw Dogs!*" we yell, in a drunken version of unison.

*

Later. At least twenty-four hours later and we haven't stopped. A cavernous hallway. The hundreds of people bathed in pink are angels. There could be a hundred or a thousand of them. All of them have marble faces. Gowns in flowing colours. Door upon door opening, they welcome us into the fold. The cotton of my dress has never felt so sensual, the skin on the palms of the hands I am shaking is the softest

I have ever touched.

A portrait hangs dead centre of the main wall; a naked man standing in the middle of a forest. The figure's mouth turns at the edges, but it's difficult to distinguish whether this expression, in the midst of this isolation, is ecstasy or darker. Adam or mad-man. I can't tell. You never can.

Reflexive images replay. The inner camera. Dead *Straw Dogs*. Champagne into vodka. Ashok fucking a girl from behind on the dance floor. Alcohol. Speed. Ecstasy. MDMA. Nicotine. Grass. Cocaine.

Finding the party. Losing the party. Running, running, running. Another high down a back alley. Racing on the street. Faces made of wax. Another high. Running away again. Ending up here. Conscious of being nobody. Finding comfort in that. Whether or not this is the same as estrangement, the man who is either lost or found in the forest, I remain unsure.

The crowd has the savage grace that comes with super affluence. Veronica works the room while Rose and I take pills in the corner. The elation from whatever I took earlier is starting to wear off. I need more. The love is dribbling away with time and so shadows set in. Again, time.

"That guy," Rose says, pointing to a bald man, "Is worth three billion. Dollars."

We're handed two cocktails by a waiter who is fussily dressed in a white tuxedo.

"Three billion dollars," I repeat. What must that look like? A money tree. No, a money mountain. "Three billion dollars. From what?"

"I don't know. Packaging. He did tell me but..." She wanders off, mid-sentence, and starts talking to a blonde man I don't recognise.

Three Billion Dollar Baldie taps his glass. There is a rippling cheer. A hush falls.

"It's great to see so many friends here tonight." He speaks with a South African twang. "As you know, I only throw parties once a year, so I have to make sure everyone has a damn good time. But there's plenty more entertainment for us here. Right now, in fact. So enjoy yourselves!"

There are whoops from the guests. Four dancers wearing trench coats appear on a platform under the arch of the ceiling. They gyrate to saxophone and sex lyrics.

I'm going to misbehave tonight, it feels all right. Wouldn't you want to take me home? Wouldn't you want to take me home?

Swaying against each other in a line, they shimmy forward. They then open and close the coats, once from the right shoulder and once from the left, much to the appreciation of the assembled crew. Removing the coats completely, they grin and swivel them at Three Billion Dollar Baldie before tossing them on the floor. Clad in PVC underwear and thigh high boots, they form another line facing away from the audience and let rip with solo spots.

One does a cat move, the next a nursemaid, then a dominatrix. The mermaid flips her legs as a tail and they all gyrate for one last time, arms aloft, as the crowd roars. They turn and shake their arses at the audience then disperse to do the mwah-mwahing. Eager men, jacked up on whatever, approach them from all angles.

Me and Veronica watch as Cat Girl defends herself against the wandering hands of an elderly guy with liver spots flecked on his forehead.

"What did you make of the dancing?" Veronica says.

"I couldn't do it. But I don't reckon anybody is going to be asking any time soon, so it's not a major concern."

"You could do it!"

Cat Girl manages to prise her coat from the arthritic fingers, running to safety beside the rest of the troupe. The elderly man tries to pursue but gives up halfway across the room, clutching his chest.

"It's not really my deal. I have two left feet, anyway. What about you?"

"Me?" Veronica says. "I don't have to work."

*

At about seven am, I come across a couple fucking doggy-style on top of my coat in a bedroom and so am in no position to leave. Turning back into the hallway, I notice Rose crouched on the floor talking into her phone.

"Don't call this number again. Do you get it?"

Rose puts her phone away and notices me standing there.

"Everyone's getting their jollies on now," I tell her, sinking down next to her. Her eyes, normally alive with mischief, have no sparkle.

"Are you all right?" I ask.

"Fine," Rose says, flatly, jumping to her feet.

Back in the cavern, a woman in a ball gown lies on the floor and starts to tear at her clothes. "I want them OFF!" she shouts. Her girlfriend picks her up and carries her out.

Enclosed again in the dreamland celebration of nothing, only the noise of voices fills the vacuum. All of them seem loud enough to have something interesting to say.

Another girl with saucer eyes offers us acid. Acid makes me even more paranoid than usual. Do I really want to spend four days indoors because my face looks *too weird* to go outside again? No. Alcohol is probably the way forward.

A man-shaped doll is positioned on top of a makeshift altar that has – I don't know how – been erected on the platform. Incense has been lit.

"If you ever, if you ever," Three Billion Dollar Baldie slurs into the microphone, "if you ever gave a fuck, here's the fellow to tell you not to give a fuck! All hail Devine!"

"All hail Devine!" the congregation shouts.

A line forms. A cluster of people get on their knees, praying to the man-doll.

"All hail Devine," they chant, over and over again.

Most of them seem hypnotised. They are believers now. Believers in the Three Billion Dollar Man. Perhaps I should get down and join them?

I waver before the altar. I don't want to worship. A figure in a white robe sleeping on the floor catches my eye. I should make friends with the angel, surely?

Sitting down next to him, I find that it's no angel. It's a local boy. He can't be over thirteen and is holding a white candle that has long since gone out. Wax has dripped on his cloak, which splits to reveal flashes of school uniform underneath. For a second, I am disappointed. Then, aware.

"What are you doing?" I ask the boy.

"I'm a prop."

Around the room, I can see several other figures slumped on the floor in Klan robes. I hadn't noticed them all night.

"Why?"

"I want a new computer game." The boy closes his eyes again. His drowsiness is catching. I follow him.

*

By the time I leave, the sky is drizzling rain. *Salut* forever, coat, gone forever to the bobbing bottoms of whoever-it-was. The fever pitch of the day has been and gone while we danced. Sobriety kicks in. The KKK took my party away.

I wish I didn't take everything so seriously. But, once an earnest writer type, always an earnest writer type. And the context requires an earnest writer response.

About context: it is everything.

"Where are you going?" a voice calls after me. I turn around; Veronica.

"Home," I shout back.

"Where is your new place?"

"It's a bit out of the way," I reply, "in Minhang." It's not a place, it's a hostel. I'm too proud to tell her that. A cab stops beside her and she opens the door.

"Come on! It's cold. You stay at my place," she says. "I have to go to Hong Kong in a couple of hours. I don't know where Rose is."

Easily persuaded, I get in the backseat with her.

"What's in Minhang? Is it the real China?" she asks, laughing at her own joke.

"It's cheap and I'm broke."

"I see."

At least she stops laughing. The car whizzes through backstreet shortcuts. The drizzle is gaining force and turning into rain.

"What do you do all day?" I ask her, as we pull up to her flat block. "You said you don't have to work."

"I do what I like."

The taxi stops.

"Don't be stupid," she says, when I try to pay. "Come on."

She puts her arm around me, almost maternal. For the first time in a long while, I'm safe.

*

I wake up in Veronica's spare, spare room still fully dressed. My head is being slowly caved in by a persistent claw hammer on the left hand side. Prostrate and with eyes wide open, it takes several minutes before I can sit upright.

Downstairs, Rose's abandoned pair of shoes by the front door indicate she must be in here. Padding barefoot into the kitchen, I locate a jar on the counter that says coffee on the front but has tea in it. As the kettle starts to boil up, Rose shuffles in wearing her pyjamas. Pink and yellow daisies are skewed in her hair at eccentric angles.

"Tea?" I ask, holding out a mug.

She takes it from me and shuffles away, her head bowed. I follow her into the living room and we collapse on the sofa.

"What happened last night?" I say, when the powers of speech have returned.

"The last thing I remember is having gin and doing selfies in a flower shop with Three Billion Dollar Baldie's BFF," she says, closing her eyes and resting the mug against her cheek. "After that I think I came straight back."

Even the vibrations that start emanating from Rose's pocket have a butterfly effect on the thudding in my skull. I cover my head with a blanket as she answers the phone. Everything is okay under the blanket – until Rose tugs at my foot.

"Leave me alone!" I mutter through the weave but she pulls it off my back, pushing my chin up.

"Roman," she mouths. It's the third time he's called her.

The hangover forgotten, I get to my feet.

"I know, I'm worried too," Rose's voice shifts in a hammy quiver.

She puts her hand over the cover of the phone and mouths at me. I don't get it. She mouths it again. I still don't get it. I find a pen wedged between the sofa cushions and hand it to her.

He wants to call Interpol! She writes on the back of an empty fag packet. I take the pen from her and write underneath.

Tell him they're already on it.

She starts to laugh but manages to turn it into a convincing cough.

"How about we leave Interpol for a few days? I'm sure she's all right. Yeah. Bye." She puts the phone down.

"God, he's a nightmare. It's…" she checks her watch, "Eleven am on a fucking Sunday! He withheld the number again."

"Perhaps I should speak to him."

"No. Don't even think about him. He's a manipulative shit."

*

Pops reminds me of the cafe I worked at in Edinburgh for a couple of months. Until I got fired for consistently messing up orders, never being on time and 'contravening health and safety legislation' by smoking beside the bins.

At the table behind Rose, a couple of Goths are in a heated discussion. Two boys with bongos finish their set as we order. A handclap echoes from all the patrons, save the Goths.

"Ashok said he can get me an audition in Chongqing. It's this movie about extra-terrestrials. They're casting for a fifth leading actress," Rose says.

"I didn't realise you were friends again," I say. "What does fifth leading actress mean?"

I follow her gaze to an elderly lady who is going through the rubbish outside.

"It means they don't think you're very talented, but that a member of the production team probably fancies you."

We are distracted from the elderly lady by the arrival of two bacon sandwiches.

"You know," Rose says, as I smother mine with ketchup, "I went to Hollywood for a year when I was nineteen. I couldn't cut it. It was horrible. The most isolated I've ever felt. Everyone was plastic-faced. I learned how to play it, but I obviously wasn't great at that either."

"Why do you want to be famous?" I bite into the sandwich. "It strikes me as a sure-fire path to insanity. That's assuming we're not there yet, of course."

"Immortality," Rose says. She takes the top slice of bread off her sandwich. "I'm watching the carbs," she adds, by way of explanation.

As she brings the half-wich to her mouth, the bacon tumbles onto the plate.

"There is a reason that there are two bits of bread," I tell her, laughing. She giggles and replaces the top piece.

"You ever wonder what Andy Warhol would have made of it here?" she says.

"He'd have loved it. Can you imagine? All the freaks, easy living, random art, nonsense, absolute disconnection from, well, normal life."

Normal life, where everyone's opinions are instantly available and you carry the world in you pocket. Where if you don't want to be in on the globe's constant status update well, sorry, but there's something wrong with you.

I think about the things that I don't want to do. To scheme or to be a proprietor of anything. Anything at all. I just want to float, like Veronica.

*

The butterfly flew to the river. She was not thirsty but she wanted to see water, to hear the lapping noise that she found so soothing. Hovering by the surface, she noticed a vision looking back at her. She moved closer. Was it Red Admiral?

Only when her legs got wet did she realise that she was Red Admiral. As she admired her reflection, she was again filled with wonder. For what the elements were and were not. For what they could create.

Twenty-three

Counting on my fingers, I realise that it has been two weeks since I checked into the *Garden of Zen* youth hostel. The dulcet tones of the owners' cats shagging in the flowerbed outside filter through the window into the room where I write at a desk. This occurs in a relentless rhythm in the early morning and again around midnight, usually lasting for at least the length of a coffee-cigarette break. As the dance of seduction and capitulation continues, I chew my pen and realise I don't know how to finish this sentence.

A new build that must have been constructed with the intention of housing a family of ten, the walls don't offer much insulation against the spring breeze. The dark wood floor creaks underfoot as I shuffle downstairs. The two other residents that I have seen, one American and one German, are in the middle of conversation on the veranda.

"What if my wife sees it on YouTube?" the American says in a panic.

"Does your vife Google stuff like 'Hot Asian Pussy'?" comes Germany's response.

Good morning. I skip out of the porch and onto the pathway that leads to the clump of shops on this block of Minhang Road. To the west, trees are showing buds of blossom in the nearby park. I plan how to spend my daily budget of seven *renminbi*. It's enough to purchase one packet of cigarettes, a boiled egg in soy sauce and rice for about five *kuai*. With the remaining two *kuai* I will buy a beer or save for a metro ticket.

While being poor requires a more strategic approach to life than I would like, it does enable you live fully in the present. There are no plans, because there is nothing to make them with. There is only putting one foot in front of the other.

I reach the gate of the complex. This area of Shanghai is dead of tourists; the suburban sprawl has proven an eerie contrast to the inner city. The cars that pass are people-carriers containing children travelling to and from the nearby private school, or suits attacking the rush hour.

When I reach the line of shacks on Minhang Road, the grocer shoots a smirk at me. As the days have gone by, the princess-treatment I received at first has dwindled to indifference.

I point to the mounds of peanuts and rice lying in sacks beside the scales, then pick out the beer I like. He picks a boiled egg out of the pot of soy sauce without prompt. I give him over my seven *kuai* and we've done our business for the day.

*

I've been in the park staring at this blank page for over two hours. I know what the story is, that much is true. I know where it is going, even if it doesn't come off that way. But getting the ending down on paper seems an impossibility, despite all the do-or-die.

I pull my books together and make my way up the path towards the lily pond.

At the water's edge, the roots trail beneath the surface.

I let my fingers glide over the rough edges of the roots until they start to get pruney. The roots are the inspiration for the flower. Where are mine? Did I mislay them along with several disastrous 'career moves', failed romances and fanciful behaviour? I don't know anymore. Perhaps inspiration, the currency of one's imagination, must also be earned.

*

The butterfly flew away from the river. She could see the city in the distance, but she could not find it in herself to go back there. While she had lost her wonder at the smells of the leaves, the humid depth of the air, the grass, she felt that this was not such a bad thing. A sense of home was keeping her in the forest; it was comfort to her in solitude.

As she flew back to the tree, the butterfly encountered a dusky odour mingled with the particles of water. It clung to her wings. Shaking them off, she turned to see a shape in the distance. The butterfly could not believe what she was seeing. It was Red Admiral.

Twenty-four

I call Joe, the Film Producer, from the *Garden of Zen*, in an attempt to find work. During the course of our short conversation he makes four bad jokes, after which he says "Kidding!" each time. I try not to dwell on this I make my way down to Taikang Road.

The smell of slow-cooked meat as I turn the corner of the lane and see *Woody's Diner* already makes the trip worthwhile. Stepping inside, I clock Joe waiting at a table and barking into his phone. He sees me straight away and waves me over. As I wait for him to finish his conversation, I peruse the jukebox-shaped menu and attempt to avoid salivating too obviously.

"And tell her to teach Maddie how to cook," he tells the person at the other end of the line. "The girl has to learn. Steak, potatoes. Proper food."

Joe hangs up the phone. His lips stretch towards his ears in what I suppose must be considered a smile.

"You're a difficult woman to get hold of!" he booms. "I called that number you gave me and spoke to your friend, Rose. She wanted a part in one of my movies?"

I bite my bottom lip.

"Rose is a very talented actress."

"Is she hot?"

"Well…" I squirm in my seat.

"Kidding! Anyway, I wanted to meet you about my film. By the way, what kind of a hippy asshole doesn't have a cell phone? *Kidding!*"

Joe slams the jukebox-shaped menu shut and beckons the waitress over.

"You can't beat a burger, can you? Fifteen years abroad and I can't kick the habit. I'm a dumb American!" The waitress takes our orders.

I pretend not to notice when Joe checks out her arse as she walks to the kitchen.

"So let me tell you about *Tree People*. It hasn't been in development long, only about five years. If you want to write, I could make things happen for you. I've got connections. I wouldn't be able to pay you, but it would be a fantastic opportunity." He slurps on his shake. "It's a tear-jerker. The story is about children who live in trees. Something happens to the children. I don't know what it is, yet. I've been thinking lately that one of them should get cancer. Do you know how I feel about cancer?"

The same as how everyone in the world feels about cancer?

"Cancer is terrible!" Joe bellows, with the zeal of a Hasidic Jew attempting to convert a Fundamentalist Mormon.

If I'd ever doubted, there is definitely no such thing as a free lunch.

*

Once we've finished eating, Joe bounds to an office that lies to the left of the café. Reluctantly, I follow him. He has babbled about *Tree People* for a full hour without interruption. Despite casting me as a human sounding board, he still isn't sure what should happen to make a plot occur although he has a lot of ideas because he's an *ideas guy*.

"What do you think?" Joe asks, marching ahead.

"There isn't much of a story to, well, think about," I reply, before I can stop myself.

The only items in Joe's headquarters that indicate its purpose are posters for two films, *Run, Baby, Run*, and *Surfacing Shanghai*. Both have photos of a redheaded teenage boy in the centre who manages to come across as awkward despite heavy airbrushing.

"My son Lenny. He's a big star!"

Joe's face drips with perspiration as he shows me clippings about Lenny taken from broadsheets, tabloids and a couple of periodicals. He leads me into the side office, complete with the leather sofa and flat-screen television.

"What would you do to get ahead?" he says, his eyes searching my chest area for a hint of a cleavage. I almost want to wish him luck.

There will be no 'producer's sofa' treatment for me. I step towards the door, but Joe blocks my path. He places a palm on my right buttock. As attempted sexual assaults go, this is small fry. I remove his hand and slap him .

Joe's shoulders sag as plonks down on the sofa, clutching his face.

"Good luck with *Tree Children*," I call out as I peg it into the corridor. "But I'd think about ditching the cancer thing."

*

The girl at the *Garden of Zen* reception desk doesn't look up from her computer game when I slip back in. On the veranda, a blonde man has taken up all of the space at the picnic table that is usually deserted. Settling on the bench that offers an outlook onto the unZen-like garden, I scoff peanuts and open a beer while inwardly vowing that one day I will detox. One glorious day.

The blonde man has wide-set eyes that give his expression an air of constant amazement. Dents of heavy living are highlighted by the shadows on his cheeks cast from the lamps. My guess is that he's around forty.

Feeling my stare, he glances up.

"Would you like to sit here?" I detect a British accent.

The table in front of him is spread with detritus. Two notebooks stuffed with more paper than it is possible for a human being to have use for at any one given time lie with the spines broken. Half a glass of wine. An over-full ashtray filled with rain water.

Pleasantries are exchanged. I learn that his name is Tony and decide that he is handsome in an astonished kind of way.

"I hate small talk," he says, pouring more wine into his glass and puffing on a cigarette.

"So do I."

I'm all small-talked out.

"I like you already." He speaks brusquely, as one who is used to having too many thoughts to be held in at any one time. "Let's assume we're friends from the fact that we're both British and lost in China."

"Deal."

"I come from Manchester. I've been here for a month but I'm staying for three. I've come to work on a project and then I will leave and go back to Britain. I miss my wife and kids. My favourite food is lasagne and my favourite film is *Last Tango in Paris*. Your turn."

"I'm between plans right now." I am aware of how silly this is as soon as I've said it.

"Well, you're the kind of go-getter I wouldn't expect to meet in a youth hostel."

"Ruthlessly ambitious."

I notice the ink stains that are now circling the wooden top of the table. "You are a writer, aren't you?"

"Yes," he mutters. "Yes, I am one of those." Self-apologists of the world unite!

"What are you working on?"

"A book. Please don't get excited," Tony says. "It's a horribly boring book. It's what the company likes to call a 'luxury travel guide'. To Shanghai. For..." he stumbles over the sentence, "'People who know how to spend money correctly'. It's a meaningless phrase, I know. But that's what the brief is."

"I didn't know there was a way to spend money correctly." Money, I've come to realise, isn't a problem. It's a solution.

"Most of the time it's just good to have it in the first place. The next installment is due tomorrow. I've been trying to churn it out. But all I really want to do is write poetry. Anyway, do you ever think this country is well... a bit tricky, for want of a better word? All this up and down, backwards coming forwards. *Guanxi.*"

"Shanghai's the sixties and the seventies and the eighties all rolled in one. Or at least that's what the *Time Out* guide says."

The moon is making an unusual appearance in the middle of the sky. Tony starts to write in his notebook but quickly gives up, casting the pen back aside.

"Nada. Nothing. Not a sausage," he says, waving at the girl inside who, disturbed from her computer game, glares at us with loathing but eventually drags herself outside to take our order.

"She must surely have professional potential in whatever the hell she's playing by now," he says, as the girl slips back and locates a bottle from under the check-in desk. She brings it over and bangs it down in front of us.

"Service with a smile, eh?" he says, pouring a glass.

"So you're a poet staying in a shitty youth hostel, writing a book about how to spend money?"

Tony's cigarette fizzles as he douses it in the ashtray. "I write modernist-style verse that's obviously not modernist. I've only ever completed two poems in my life that I actually like."

"I guess the chances of you showing me them are slim?"

"Don't take it personally."

"Cheers," I reply. He holds up his glass and I clink it with my beer bottle. Looking up at the moon, I can't help but feel heartened by the fact that for once my life seems less ridiculous than somebody else's.

*

The next morning, I watch the goldfish moving in the Zen garden's fountain. There can't be much oxygen in the water; they keep poking their mouths out. Weeds entangle themselves with the bodies. Tony, green in the face, emerges through the double doors.

"What time were we out here till?" he says, pulling up a wicker chair with an effort.

"I have no idea," I reply. "Tell me, do you get lonely?"

"What we do is lonely. It's all in your head or in your hands. There's not much in between. And writing is re-writing. So it's a profession in which self-flagellation is part of the daily norm."

The sun is out now, clearing a path through the sky and smog to shine directly onto our heads.

"You started telling me about your story last night," he says. "It's about a butterfly."

I must have been gone.

"It's not a kiddy book."

"Yes, you kept saying that. I still want to read it."

"It isn't finished yet."

*

"There you are!" the butterfly said to Red Admiral.

"Follow me," he said.

"Why? I followed you before, and we lost each other."

"I can't explain, just follow me."

Still unsure, she flew after him. They came to a dank hole at the base of a tree. Red Admiral stopped. Without warning, he gripped onto the butterfly's abdomen and pulled her into the hole. She gripped him back. Instinct guided their sex.

When it was over, Red Admiral flew away, leaving the butterfly behind. Still in shock what had just happened, she knew that she would never see him again.

Twenty-five

Freddy's has squashy chairs and reasonable prices. The waitresses don't disturb you even if you sit with the same half-empty cup staring back at you for most of the day. I close the fourteenth Moleskine notebook. No genius today. If ever there were.

There are two other customers in the place. One is a young Western guy with a plate of nachos, the other is a very thin middle-aged Chinese lady who has been nursing a cream cake for over an hour, apparently unable to finish it but unwilling to leave it either. As I ponder the less-discussed merits of masochism again, Rose clatters down on the seat opposite me on her phone. Another new dress. This one is bright orange.

"It's not possible now," she says. While she covers her mouth with her hand, her voice is trained to carry and remains fully audible. "I didn't tell him. Most of the talking was on the phone. You think it'll... Okay. Okay."

She ends the call and reaches into her bag, pulling out the script for *Alien Predator 3*.

"It's three lines and dying from asphyxiation, but we don't have to worry about that bit," she says, pointing to the highlighted dialogue for Fifth Alien Predator's Assistant.

Although I don't know much – or indeed anything – about acting, after half an hour of going through it even I can tell Rose is having an off-day. On the seventh read-through, she still can't get the lines right.

"I can't concentrate," she says, taking the script back.

"How's Veronica?" I ask, stretching.

"She's gone out of town again."

Groping in her handbag, she grabs a cigarette. Her hands fumble with the lighter. It takes a few sparks before the flame holds. Through the smoke, her eyes slip over to the TV screen behind me. An earthquake rescue operation. It's two weeks since it happened and families are still searching for the bodies of their relatives.

"All those poor people, and there's nothing we can do," Rose says.

A rescuer pulls at a body wedged in rubble. It isn't obvious whether it's a man or a woman, what its features resemble. Even that it was once a person. The footage cuts to the agonised faces of the waiting loved-ones as they in turn watch from a screen in a rescue centre. Most of them video the screen with smartphones. Camera upon screen upon camera.

"There's nothing we can do about an earthquake sitting on our arses in a café, no," I reply, one of the more pragmatic sentences I have ever uttered.

Rose frowns in an effort to hold in tears. I pass her a napkin. I should never say anything about anything. To anybody. Particularly sensitive actress types.

A smooth news reporter comes on and explains that it's the body of a woman in her thirties, Shen. A photo of Shen at her friends' house flashes up. As if to remind us that this beaten up body did once laugh and enjoy life.

"All those poor people," Rose says again, wiping her cheeks.

Thankfully, the television switches to a South Korean soap opera. Once the opening credits have rolled, a couple starts having an argument which switches to a kiss so melodramatic that it is hard to stomach even when doing level best to maintain a semblance of laconic detachment. I giggle at Rose. Nothing. Apprehension winds from my stomach towards the back of my throat.

"I had a massive credit card bill," she blurts out. "Like, ten thousand dollars. It was an old card and... oh, whatever. I'd been leaving it for ages because I was screwed. I didn't know what to do. I've been getting all these emails from bank... And one night, I got upset. I was in the living room. I woke Veronica up. See that?" she says, pointing to the screen.

The woman who was kissing the male lead in the previous scene is now standing over his dead body with a bloody kitchen knife, laughing.

"Funny," I say.

"Veronica," Rose says, her eyes falling from the television. "I told her everything. And she says, I can see you're tight. I know how you can make a bit of money."

"Doing what?"

She takes a deep breath. "Do I really have to spell it out?"

We hold each other's eyes for a minute. I drop mine first.

Rose lights a fresh cigarette from the end of the old one. The tears stop. She is beyond the invisible barrier.

"What was it like?" As soon as the words come out of my mouth, I hate myself for asking. Writer first. Human being second. The young Western man stops eating his nachos and inches his seat closer to our table. I'd be eavesdropping if it were me. I give him that.

"Not here," Rose says.

I want to hug her but the inward-turned shape of her shoulders gives the impression that she doesn't want to be touched.

"I'm a fucking joke," comes her cold self-assessment. "I can't act. If I could, I wouldn't be Fifth Alien Predator's Assistant. The reality is, if I was going anywhere I would be doing it, and in LA or London. I'm just not very good. I suppose if there's a purpose, if it's not an end in itself, it's not any worse than going to an office for five days a week and realising you've lost your mind in forty years. At least with this, the madness is brash and loud and you know it's happening."

All this she says with the dispassion of someone who has accepted that their dream will not work out, that they are not exceptional, that they aren't doing anything above the norm or that can't be done by the person the next table over a good deal better.

Rose conceding that her path in life may not have been the right one, without much fight or bluster, is seeing the lioness sedated and ready for skinning.

*

As we reach the *Garden of Zen*, a tabby wanders lethargically across the patio. Rose tugs at my arm.

"Do you think I'm a bad person?"

"There's not really bad or good," I say, as we make our way up the steps. "There's just what you choose to do with your time. And what do you care what I think? I'm nobody."

"You're a nobody whose face is hanging in an art gallery."

"But..."

I lose the sentence because I don't know how to end it.

None of that was real.

None of this is.

In the lobby, the girl at the front desk is again immersed in her computer game. We reach my room. Mindless, Rose shuffles onto the bed. I take my shoes off and fill a couple of glasses with beer.

"I suppose it's not the sort of thing you should ideally be doing with yourself," I say, handing her one.

"An ideal world. Let's not talk about it because we don't live in one. I've done acting jobs than have been a lot more embarrassing and a lot worse paid," she says, without humour. "I try to think about it like that. At least with sex there's a predictable climax. Whether it's real or not. In the end, you get up and leave and you never have to see each other again."

She takes a gulp of beer.

"Four times it's been, now. Twice the full... Sex. For local girls it's nothing. But for blonde hair and big tits – big bucks, especially from Mainland Chinese. We're unusual. The last time I did it, I didn't even have to do much. But..." she says, the bleakness in her eyes like nothing I have seen before or would wish to see again. "My hands are getting dirty. Do you know what I mean?"

She puts the glass on the side table and fiddles with the blanket on top of the bed. Twisting the blanket in her fingers, she knots and unties the fraying edges. She replaces it and irons it down again with the palm of her right hand, then picks it up. She knots, unties and flattens. She does it over and over.

"I went to this house. The guy, Wim, he gets his kicks from being watched. I have to tell you about it. I have to tell you about it because I have no peace."

She sinks back on the bed and gazes up at the ceiling.

"Veronica was kind of curt with me on the way there. The drive takes a long time, although it's not far from her place; the traffic is bad. We pull up at the house, off Huaihai Road. It reminds me of a villa in France. I'm first struck by how good-looking Wim is. I was surprised, you know? We go inside. The house smells of lavender. Like your grandparents. It was so peculiar, you know?"

I don't know. The room takes on a new texture with her words as she vanishes in the relief of confession.

"They are chatting in German. The pictures on the walls; abstract square things. Cream furniture. Everything white, perfect. Wim goes into the kitchen to get the drinks. Veronica asks me if I'm okay. Of course, I tell her I'm fine. She gives me coke. I go to the bathroom. The line does nothing to prop me up. When I get back, they are still talking in German. Wim tries to talk to me, but he's not that comfortable speaking in English so I let it drop. I keep fixating on the painting above the fireplace. Red and black squares. Like if I remember it, or I focus on it really hard, it will take this all away. They start to kiss. A kind of romance spectacle. He puts his hands on her. Up her skirt.

"Wim tries to pull me in. Veronica, she has told him to call her Ms. V tonight. That's the name she uses with clients when she's being a dominatrix. She tells Wim not yet. He says yes, mistress. She stands up, clicks her fingers. Wim follows her. She told me before what she was gonna do. I go after them. He gets on the bed. She tells him to take her clothes off. Underneath is all latex. Proper hardcore. She tells him to get down. I stand in the corner."

I try to disconnect. The world is research. I want to cry for her. But I can't cry. For her.

"He gets on the bed. Wait, I already said that. They start, I pretend I am watching a film. A very real kind of film. She starts to slap him, whip him, all of that. He gets excited.

"Mercy, mercy, he says. Over and over again. The more he begs the

148

more turned on he gets. He asks me - have I been bad? Veronica hits him again. I'm gonna make you sorry, she says. I'm gonna make you so sorry. No mistress, he says. She keeps hitting him. His arse is getting red. He keeps trying to turn to me. But she gags him. Whispers in his ear. She keeps saying that I don't want him. That nobody wants him, that he is shit. And he is so turned on. He yells and moans. Louder and louder. I make like I'm touching myself, but I'm standing in the corner and I'm waiting for it to be over."

She lets out a cry, faint as a dying bird.

"I'll be okay," she says, still knotting, untying and smoothing with relentless repetition. As I reach the see-through ceiling of sanity that moves you to scream, to tell someone to stop everything, she drops the blanket and curls up into the foetal position.

"Go to sleep," I tell her.

Sleep and release.

*

The butterfly's belly grew fat and full. Her flight slowed; she could not pick up speed the way that she used to. She longed to be weightless and free again, to be rid of her swollen stomach. She stopped on the grass. Taken over by another instinct, she began to push.

Twenty-six

The warmth of the spring is picking up the length of men's shirt-sleeves and chasing children indoors. Old people with dampened cloths for hats laze on folded chairs in the *longtangs*, only moving to occasionally fan themselves with newspapers. After meandering for what feels like hours, the familiarity of Suzhou Creek surges ahead. From the bridge, the city lights merge into each other, unmoved by the refrains of the night. Flies collect at the top of the river, their splashes making ripples the size of two-penny coins.

The owner of the *baokan ting* closest to the bus stop pushes an English-language newspaper out of the hatch when she sees me. I scan the front of the tabloid and try to hand it back.

"No want," the *baokan ting* seller says, putting down a half-finished infant sweater dangling from knitting needles and shaking her hand. "Yes-ta-day."

"*Xiexie,*" I tell her.

I tuck the paper under my arm and make off to find the *Bongo Lounge* where Jia Ma suggested we meet. With rare foresight, I wore canvas pumps that were on the verge of giving up the ghost. Another hip, underground gig venue, another mosh pit; another messed-up pair of shoes.

The supporting act hasn't started by the time I arrive. There's no sign of Jia Ma. I park by the bar to wait, people-watching.

A singer who introduces himself as Small Seed takes to the mic positioned by the chimney breast. He is no more than five feet, but when he sings his voice gives him weight. The tune is a merging of English and Chinese.

"*I lost you, but I found another keeper,*" Small Seed sings. "*Wo ai ni.*"

After a short set he disappears into the swell of the audience and another enigma has gone. Where the hell is Jia Ma? This is exactly the sort of situation in which having a phone would be incredibly useful.

Pulling out the newspaper, I flip through with the absent mind of one who will always intend a more thorough read later but will never get around to it. Just as I am thinking about whether I can get away with asking for another tap water, a story illustrated by a thumbnail-sized picture on the bottom left hand corner of the page catches my attention.

Hsu Xinwen, 27, was reported missing two months ago. If you have any information about his whereabouts, please contact the authorities.

"Sorry I'm so late!" Jia Ma's voice comes from beside me. I look up.

When I don't say anything, she pulls a face.

"Okay, I said I'm sorry, let me buy you a drink to make up?"

I hold out the crumpled newspaper.

"What's this?"

I point to the picture of Roman lurking in the corner of the page. Jia Ma draws her breath in sharply as she reads. Behind her, the members of the main act set up synthesisers and keyboards.

"Maybe if we put it away, it won't be real," I tell her, folding the paper in half. "People can't just disappear."

Jia Ma drops her head. "Yes, they can."

"Try his number," I tell her. Jia Ma dials.

"Disconnected," she says.

The synths build to near-deafening volume and Silver Sister's lead singer screams at the crowd in an effort to pump out energy. A few of the more die-hard fans swarm to the front. We watch for a while, but the need to be outside and alone overpowers me.

"I have to go," I tell her.

We hold hands as we walk to the station, the horror making us into little girls again. Perhaps I can regress.

"Will you be all right?" she asks.

I shrug. I can't talk to my friends. I talk to them less well than strangers. Unsure what to do, she gives me a hug. I leave her at the top of the steps. Inside, even the platform seems like a dangerous place.

"*Laowai!*" I hear a sniggering voice from my right as I stare blankly into the dark tunnel. It's coming from a group of kids, not much older than fourteen. I can't tell who the perpetrator is. The headlights of the train flash from inside the tunnel.

As the doors of the carriage slam shut and the train speeds up, I scrabble in my handbag. Finding my black beret, I slide it on, fighting the craving to be inconspicuous again.

*

Guilt proves to be a sustaining source of energy. Traversing the memories of the last time I saw Roman keeps me roaming the streets for hours. The verse-chorus-verse-chorus of inner monologue song oscillates continually between hatred and longing. Memory can be as suffocating as imagination. But what is memory, if it's not an invocation of old realities? Those that haunt you as you move so free.

Can I bring him back? Perhaps I could have forgotten.

Without intending to, I've reached the lane by Roman's studio. An elderly man is selling pineapples from a cart. The lane itself is the same, for the most part. The Xinjiang restaurant on the corner – the one indication of this patch's interaction with the world – is still there. Boys in *kufi* hats stand in white shorts. One of them kneads a bowl of dough, pausing occasionally to sprinkle sesame seeds into it. The later products of this labour, round breads, dot the industrial sized metal trays. Beside a large smoking grill, another boy puts pieces of lamb on skewers.

Past the gate, the warehouse has gone, replaced by workers, underwear and the foundations of a new complex. To the left is a rubbish dump with official signs. A mannequin's hand sticks out of the rubble. Old furniture – sofas, chairs – forms a hobo living room of sorts.

To the right, a hive of activity. An elderly woman who presumably has authority is standing next to a gas ring and a microwave. She weighs the items, judging their value. A young man in a blue workman's suit gives her cash and takes the items away. The elderly woman notices me and indicates to a dressing table. I wave her away.

Pushing past the small group, I stumble on a beaten up jewellery box. My imagination booms – I recognise it. It's Roman's. Isn't it? Maybe I can take a piece of him with me. Leaning down, I realise that I don't know the box at all.

Further in, two operatives are manning a crane lifting the scrap. It digs into a pile then deposits the objects on the other side of the dumping yard. A fire smokes in the corner, belching out a stench of burning rubber. More men in workmen's uniforms hover beside it, warming their hands.

"Foreigner!" shouts one of the workmen in English as I climb back through the gap in the fence.

The Xinjiang boys have now paused for a kick about with an old football on the corner. I glance up and down the street. Strip lights flicker from the overpass. Whenever I looked around before, I saw a proud city. All there is now is urban tumbleweed. I've got nothing to prove by staying here and being slowly devoured.

*

The butterfly did not know what to do with the jewels she had laid. She could think only of the one she had come from and her time as a caterpillar.

Leaving them on the grass, the butterfly flew away. She no longer yearned for Red Admiral. She never wanted to see him again.

Her wings felt heavier and she found that she could not fly as fast as she used to. She no longer wanted to go as high and see as far. She was starting to lose interest in the world around her, once so fresh and vivid.

Twenty-seven

The police station waiting room is noiseless, except for the hum of a television attached to a stand in the corner and the occasional burst of chatter between the two constables behind the glass booth. I sit between Rose and Jia Ma, my head in my hands. Jia Ma's earlier efforts at making light-hearted chat were met with apathy from both of us.

After three lukewarm cups of green tea, we are ushered into an interview room. We sit opposite a steel-haired Sergeant and an assistant constable. The Sergeant flashes her identity badge, the leather case decorated by a gold crest with a blood red depiction of the Forbidden City in the centre. The tick of the clock seems aggressive as the Sergeant fills in a couple of forms and examines our passports.

"I'm Sergeant Hua Shen. Sorry for the wait," she says in English. "I just wanted to confirm the details with you before I file the information. You're here on tourist visas?"

"We're travellers," Rose says, airily.

The Sergeant makes a note then looks at me.

"Hsu was your boyfriend?"

"Yes. For want of a better word," I reply.

"What?"

"Yes, he was my boyfriend."

"And when was the last time you saw him?"

"The end of February. Must have been the twenty-fifth. In Xi'an."

"Four days before he was reported missing," the Sergeant says, making a note on her form. She looks at Rose more closely.

"You spoke to Hsu, is that right?"

"Yes," Rose says. "He called a couple of times. He wanted to talk to my friend here."

"The phonecalls, when did they stop?"

"The last one was about six weeks ago," Rose says. "I told him that I didn't know where she was. Then I hung up. It was the same each time."

"Can I see the phone?"

Rose reaches into her bag and passes the phone to the Sergeant.

"They were all from a withheld number," Rose says.

The Sergeant examines the phone and passes it back, muttering to the assistant, who picks up the forms and leaves the room. While we wait, the Sergeant scribbles more onto her notepad, then puts her pen down.

"Do you like China?" she asks, the sternness softening. Do I?

"It's weird and wonderful," Rose says. The Sergeant smiles.

The assistant comes back into the room and hands Jia Ma a couple of typed pages in Chinese.

"Do you want me to translate? It's exactly what you both said," she says.

I shake my head. Rose and I sign and hand the pages to the Sergeant.

"You can go," the Sergeant says. "Enjoy the rest of your stay."

"We will," Rose says, grandly. I can't tell when she's acting anymore. We get up to leave.

"What do you think happened to him?" I ask the Sergeant. She looks at me square in the face.

"It's not my case," the Sergeant says. "My colleagues just don't know at this point. I hope we will."

"Can you let us know if you find anything?" I stumble on the question.

"Of course."

*

The vegetable market is being broken down for the evening as we make our way from the metro station. Beside the back entrance, a man tugs whole roasted chickens from spits and offers them cut price.

Jia Ma kisses us both on the cheek and leaves to go to work.

I buy lotus fruit wrapped in cellophane while Rose taps on her phone. The air is heavy with the change of the season, the shift from inward to outward. Despite her company, the now familiar mixture of loneliness and claustrophobia envelopes me.

Further down the street, we reach the *Film Café*. Pictures of glamorous stars from previous generations mixed with posters of cult movies dot the walls. We move to the back and settle into two brown leather armchairs. The waitress comes over.

"I'll just have water," I say, with as much feigned indifference as I can muster.

"Order what you like," Rose says. "It's on me."

She chooses a Salty Dog. Feeling less adventurous, I go for a Mojito and glance at an expatriate magazine. A small world, this one. Partygoers even I have met gracing the pages of the 'People' column.

"You need a proper meal and a new shirt," Rose says, grabbing a few hundred *kuai* notes from her purse. "I'll lend you money."

"I don't want it."

"You look like one of those girls in famine appeal adverts," she says, forcing them into my hand. "All bony except for the pot belly."

"Thank you," I say, swallowing hard as I shove them in my purse.

"You can't look me in the eyes anymore, can you?" she says.

"It's not about you."

She drinks the Salty Dog quickly before stretching a hand out in the direction of the waitress again. The next round arrives before I've finished my first.

"I need to leave," I tell her.

"Where will you go?"

"I don't know."

"I could have work for you," she says. "For the flight. And more."

Of course she's offering me a job. I light a cigarette. This is what it is.

"What are you, a pimp now?"

"I want to help you. I don't know about you, but I never want to feel like I owe anybody anything. You need to live. This guy has been wanting a redhead for ages. Your hair's a commodity!"

"Good to know I have a USP."

She nods. The door is there. I have legs. I can get up and walk out.

"Exactly. It's easy money for what you'd do on a wild night anyway," she says.

As she continues to talk, more to herself than to me, I know I shouldn't listen.

*

The butterfly was starting to feel that she would never experience happiness despite all that she had seen and done. The pursuit of it seemed to be just a trick that fooled everyone into acting their required parts, if only for a short while.

Flying slowly, the butterfly noticed a human body lying in the grass. Far-removed from civilisation as it was, this was not a place people tended to come. She flew closer. It was a young woman. Red hair, a yellow summer dress. The woman was unconscious. The soles of her feet arched in, a ballerina poised on tiptoe.

The butterfly perched on the dress. The woman's hand batted her away. Unabashed, the butterfly stayed where she was. The girl opened her eyes and gazed at the butterfly in wonder.

Twenty-eight

Veronica directs the cab to a new restaurant called *Shako* located near Xiangyang Road, tucked into off-street enclave that can't be seen from the main strip. The seclusion certainly fits the shiftiness that buries in my stomach. Maybe if I do this, I can eliminate the loneliness of another person? Maybe that's all it is. Maybe, maybe. More maybe.

Ever the tap dancer, as soon as we get to the table Veronica is charming the fifty-plus couple next to us. She bubbles answers to their questions about her latest happenings and parties she has attended. Is it wrong to think they're fools?

"It's good to see you," Veronica addresses me warmly, the middle-aged couple fobbed off with a dinner invitation. "We've never really talked too deeply."

"No."

A waiter in an orange boiler suit reels off specials with the reverence of a RADA undergraduate on the Pinter and produces an aged bottle of plum wine. Once Boiler Suit dashes off with our order, we have no choice but to talk with each other. I'm staring into the sun.

Veronica imparts cultural news mixed with recent events and hobnobbing. My replies are almost all monosyllabic. Having a conversation with her is so hypnotic that you almost want to avert your eyes in case your retinas burn up or you are converted for life. When she starts on the merits of the new designer boutique opening that she attended earlier that day, small talk seems even more defunct now than ever.

I might as well say it. "Shall we cut the shit?"

"Of course. I like your style."

Her face shifts into a merchant's smile. Another mercurial personality to add to Shanghai's already exhaustive list.

The waiter returns with plates of sashimi and sushi. Veronica spoons wasabi and ginger onto the side of her plate.

"It's a very wealthy man. He wants a redhead for the weekend. He's never had one. He's too rich to not have tried everything and wants to impress the other guests. He would pay you twelve thousand. Dollars. He knows of you, that this is your first time." She may as well be relaying items on a supermarket shopping list.

"Has he got a sex dungeon?"

"He may do, I don't know. But this is all because of a business thing. It's not because he's kinky, it's because he's... how you say... dirty rich?"

Language goofs: always rearing their heads at inopportune moments.

"Filthy rich."

"Yes, filthy. If you do this, you'd be set up for ages. Believe me, this is big. Afterwards, you can do what you want. You remind me a lot of myself. Restless."

I wish I could say she was wrong. Unable to contain my curiosity, I lean forward. "Why do you do it?"

Veronica raises her eyebrows. For a second it seems that she might want to leave the table. She doesn't.

"I grew up in a town an hour away from Bucharest. We had one video player in the village so we would pass it around every week. The only film we had to watch was *An American In Paris*, that musical. You know it?"

I shake my head.

"I must have seen that film seven hundred times, no exaggeration. The last time I remember watching it, I was thirteen. I could tell you it from start to finish right now. There's this line I always remember when I think about Shanghai. 'I like Paris; it's a place where you don't run into old friends'. Anyway, the point is, even then I already knew that communism, these ideals, they are... how you say... 'not all they're cracked up to be'. And I wanted to be like I am on celluloid. The whole time. Now, I do what I want when I want and I have the very best of everything."

Boiler Suit holds out a dish of pastel-coloured desserts. Veronica waves him away and drops her voice.

"The time with Rose. That was a special case. It shook her up a bit. That guy, he was screaming. He was in pain. And you know what I was thinking about?"

She offers me a cigarette. I light one and inhale so deeply my lungs burn.

"I was thinking about those fuckers from previous days. When I was much younger than you and I didn't have a clue how to take care of myself. And a lot of guys, you know, they are born to think that they can screw with women. They fucked me up, they tore me, they didn't care."

Boiler Suit arrives with the bill. Smiling at him, she is not the same person.

"He's called Goh," say says. "I think you've met. He's a good friend of mine."

"Yes." He didn't seem like that type of guy. But then, I'm not that type of girl. Except I am.

"Will you do it?" She slips a gold credit card into the leather receipt holder. For many reasons, I nod.

A couple of glamorous women request a selfie with Veronica en route to the entrance. She politely refuses. Another boiler-suited minion runs into our path to open the front door for her, as though for a member of the British aristocracy. I have to stifle a smile at their submission. If only they knew.

Outside, Veronica turns to me.

"Life is a game," she says, buttoning a jacket that probably cost more than my month's rent. "Play it with style."

*

Precision is all in the make-up. The base is a nude shade. The liquid eyeliner has a flick at the edges. I can be a cat this way. Red lips. Red for dead. Do everything silently, like a creep would. I am a creep, now.

I swirl a shot of gin around my mouth. No tonic, just bitter. It would be a good thing to have rituals. Modus operandi. As it stands, I am simply a girl in a dress. I put on a pair of heels I inherited from Rose. The higher the heel the greater the likelihood of being lifted up.

I glance around the hostel bedroom. I could stay here. But if I'm going to rot anyway, I should take the chance to leave. I pick up my handbag and the small amount of cash I have left. I owe them for this week. If I walk quickly through the lobby, chances are nobody will stop me. I switch the desk lamp off and then on again. I don't want to come back to a dark room. Not tonight.

*

I arrive at *Joules Joules* fifteen minutes early. Gold mantlepieces on either side of the entrance are matched by baize that streams from the ceiling. I make my way to the ladies' for a pick-me-up. The soap smells of roses. There is a faint flush on my face under the fluorescent bulb. I cut a line of the coke Rose gave me on the top of the cistern. Snort. And then one more for luck. Snort. This is a means to an end, not an end in itself.

Down the stairs again. Everything lighter. Brighter. I recognise a figure standing in the lobby.

"You're..." my voice cracks. What is his name? Although I've repeated it to myself what must be hundreds of times over the past few days, I draw blank.

"Goh. I'm glad to see you again."

As we walk through the dining hall, several people glance up at him. The recognition, the smiles. This is a man who matters.

When we reach the table, a bottle of wine in a cooler has already been positioned next to the vase of short-stemmed white roses. Goh clicks his fingers at the waiter who tailed us and orders.

"I come here all the time, I know the menu off by heart," he says. "We share everything."

Nervous and high, I don't know how to arrange my body in the seat and fiddle with the napkin. He doesn't seem at all affected by the context of what Veronica referred to as the 'date'. Everything about the way he moves his hands, holds his fork and adjusts the napkin on his lap suggests self-control. Whether it is instinctive or learned isn't clear.

"Your picture is hanging in my living room downtown. It's so funny to see you like this."

"Not dressed in a monkey costume?" I ask. He grins.

"I'm sorry to hear what happened to the artist," he says.

"What do you know about what happened?"

"He disappeared."

"Anything else?" I can't help it.

Goh is surprised. "They didn't find a body. They still don't know."

Detached from the surroundings, I watch him eat a plate of lobster. My hands are shaking so much that when I try to pick up a claw with my chopsticks it keeps falling through.

"Relax," Goh says, gently.

"I'm trying."

"I'm not going to ask you to come home with me tonight."

I let out the tight air that has been blocking my chest since I got here.

"Ok," I say. "Let's talk."

He tells me about his life. Becoming an apprentice at a shoemaker to help his mother with the bills. Taking over from the owner when he retired, expanding the shop to two stores. Then three. Then one in Shanghai. Then more and more. Always seeing the opportunity for growth. Travelling the world. Seeing no boundaries, only potential conquests. My reluctance gives way to enjoyment after an hour. He's a good book of a man.

"Have you and Veronica ever been together?" I ask.

"No. She's the one person I've ever met who is truly formidable. I think it comes from knowing that she never had anything to lose."

Over espressos and watermelon, he gets to the topic that has been sidestepped.

"The plan is that my partners are coming to the country house· for the weekend. We need to talk business, a project we have been working on for a decade. I want it to succeed; it will give back to China. I haven't seen one of them for four years. I thought of you because you strike me as good company. You know, yours is a very unusual beauty. You should respect it."

"It's a face thing?"

"Partly that. I'm still an insecure shoemaker from a village outside Guangzhou in my heart! So, yes. Face is important to me. I am proud."

Now I understand. Don't I?

*

The evening winds down to an easy silence as we drive to the suburbs of Minhang. This is in itself disquieting. I catch the chauffeur's eye in the rear-view mirror. I wonder if he has seen this many times before.

"Have you ever been to Lake Como?" Goh says, as the car grinds to a halt at the traffic lights.

"I didn't make it, no."

"I have a workshop there. When you are in Italy, you must come!"

I giggle. Jesus. It's as though we're on an actual date. The chauffeur pulls up at the crossing nearest the *Garden of Zen*. I get out of the car.

"I'll see you tomorrow, then," Goh says, leaning through the half-open window. "We'll pick you up at eleven am."

As the wind balloons up my skirt, the chauffeur drives off before I can say goodbye.

*

"Am I dreaming you, or are you dreaming me dreaming you?" the woman asked the butterfly.

Although disconcerted by the question, the butterfly liked the awkwardness with which the woman spoke. They examined each other. For the first time in her life, the butterfly felt sleepy. She had never felt so tired.

x

Twenty-nine

We pull up at a shopping centre I have passed several times but never entered. I admire Goh's straight back from behind as we walk to the Chanel shop. Inside, the sole other customer is a woman carrying a little dog in her handbag. She's strutting the way a woman struts on a sunny day when they know they look good.

I pick up a mini-dress in hounds tooth print, nothing too sexy. Goh examines it, takes it from me and puts it back on the rack without comment. I am not going to argue.

His body language is more jagged than the lubricated evening last night as he rummages through garments. Eventually, he selects a red ball gown with gold sequins on it. I want to tell him it will clash with my hair but I hold off. Better to go along with his fantasy, I suppose.

Muzak from the main area of the shop filters from behind the white curtains as I get changed. If this were a romcom, an upbeat theme tune would be building up in the background right now. The audience would think that the girl will fall in love with the man who has selected the dress. The ugly man with money. The lone wolf.

Goh asks if he can take a look. Before I can answer, he pulls back the curtain.

"That's the one," he says. He drops the curtain again.

At the register he has lined up a few more items on the counter. As he reaches into his wallet, I notice how neat his hands are. The nails are filed and square-shaped. The nails of a person who is used to getting his hands dirty and having them cleaned by somebody else.

"*Xiexieguanglin!*" the assistant says, handing the bag to him. Is it my imagination, or does her voice hold a wistfulness? She probably thinks we are lovers. Goh picks up the bag and strides out of the shop towards the car.

Within minutes we are on the Yan'an elevated highway. The car's speed quickly picks up on the straight stretch of road, the overhead lamps lending a fluorescent hue to downtown.

Valium gives everything a softer edge. This lapse in control will mean control. Fuzzy logic. Is it happening? Billboards and advertisements flash by. The TV screens in people's homes. They are happening. Typing your dead books may feel like an out.

Books: happening.

Goh makes calls. The wheels of the car keep on turning. As we drive on, I indulge a hope that the roads might levitate instead of elevate.

*

I've entered the twilight zone.

Mental amendment: that was probably a while ago.

The style of the mansion and its thatched roof seems inspired by the cottages of rural England except on a bigger scale. This is only undermined by a twenties-style porthole that overlooks the driveway three floors up. We are met by a servant dressed in a powder-blue uniform. She reaches into the back of the car and pulls out the trunk Goh brought. I try to take one of the handles to help. The servant glances at me with such surprise I let go straight away.

The staircase in the hallway sweeps up. Towards the back, patio doors give way to open loungers propped beside the swimming pool, jacuzzi and tennis court, beyond which lies a lake. In another world, this would be a kind of paradise.

"I have to do some work." Given that he barely spoke in the car, the boom of Goh's voice is jarring. "Wu Yi will show you where to go."

He gestures to the *ayi* and disappears down the hallway to the right, which is hung with watercolour paintings of classical Chinese figures. Wu Yi leads me up the stairs to a bedroom at the end of the first floor hallway.

A time jump from the exterior, it is filled with eighteenth century baroque-style furniture. The four-poster bed is smothered in red silk. Two floor-to-ceiling windows give one view onto the pool and lake, and another of the winding driveway on the opposite side.

"First I give you massage," Wu Yi says.

I remove my clothes and don a black silk robe that's laid out. I follow Wu Yi into a den leading off from the bedroom, which is connected to a vast ensuite bathroom. Lined with candles, it hums with piped music.

I put my head through the hole of the massage bed, watching her feet below. She pushes on my shoulders, curving her fingers down my spine and the back of my neck. I turn over and she puts a pack on my face that smells of cucumber and aloe. As the pack soaks in, she rubs another cream all over the rest of my body and sloughs off the dead skin with a mitten before rinsing my face.

"Turn back." Grey curls of skin decorate the floor.

She massages the base of my neck. Knots, knots. Everything is knots.

"Tense, tight," she says.

She pours liquid on my back. A sour smell rises as it dries, penetrating my nostrils. She leaves the room. Anxiety has depleted. The wordless music washes into my head. Into the parts that can't be touched. What feels like hours later, she comes back in and taps me on the shoulder. I get up. The robe glides on so smoothly I could be skinless.

A black silk dress is laid out on the bed. Wu Yi turns away as I put it on. I don't want a mirror. Better to leave it to the imagination. In the future, this weekend will all have been a dream anyway. Nothing more.

There is a knock: Goh. Although I can see him reflected in the window, I don't turn around. Wu Yi bows to us both and leaves.

"The guests will be arriving soon," he says. "My business associates and their girlfriends."

"Concubines?" Playing with fire. I want to be burnt.

Goh comes closer and watches me put the shoes on. There are elegant but fierce; shoes of aspiration, then. These are shoes that could take you to the moon and bring you back, laughing.

"Did you make these?"

"Yes. Remember you haven't got the money yet. Keep your mouth shut unless it's to say pleasant things. You did agree to be here."

The door bangs shut behind him. A warped bride-to-be, I take as long as possible with my make-up, getting it just so. I don't tie my hair up; more to hide behind.

By the time I get downstairs, the guests are being served drinks and canapés in the lounge area. Numb, I shake hands as names are exchanged. Xi Wei and Rosemary, Gu Feng and Lily, Lei Fu and Jenny. There are no comments about my lateness.

The sight of the lake in the falling sun offers a visual breath outside of the cloistered atmosphere. I could jump in, let it drag me to its depths. But Goh's right: I chose this. I have to suck it up.

The associates are all men dressed in tuxedos. Their girlfriends' faces are pale, the pores buffed into virtual non-existence. They all have great hair and perfect bodies. It quickly becomes apparent that a major source of their conversation is best practise in the maintenance of both. Will I remember which one is which at the end of the evening? Unlikely.

Rosemary and Lily are both from Beijing and Jenny is from Hong Kong. I make chitchat with Jenny about her cat, Mitzy. Jenny talks about Mitzy for so long I manage to drink three glasses of champagne straight. The edge has been removed, at least for the time being. Mitzy's life becomes more involving.

A bell rings and we move through one of the downstairs halls to the dining room at the end. Owing a debt to Louis the Sixteenth, the table is laid with long white candles in silver holders; each place is set with silver chopsticks and goblets. Goh sits at the head of the table. I sit at the other end, next to Xi Wei. Servants dash to replenish our goblets. Shark's fin soup, whole suckling pig, crab stuffed with abalone and lobster are served.

I pick at a piece of suckling pig as the conversation flows mostly in Mandarin. I should be in the moment. The moment that is not now. Time is a resource and it runs out. It doesn't come back. You can't make up more. An exclusive part, one piece, should be saved for the people I love.

"I'm planning to go to Tiger Leaping Gorge next weekend," Jenny says in English from the seat next to Goh, seeming to address me.

"Perhaps we can join you," I say, knowing that this will not happen. May as well keep up a degree of showmanship.

The servant clears our plates and gives us fresh ones, but I find I'm already full. Xi Wei turns away from the long conversation he has been having with Lily on his left hand side and addresses me in English.

"We're all working on the *Meng Zhi Cheng*." Xi Wei's tone suggests that this, in my position of girl with Goh, is something I should know about. I make a non-committal noise.

"What about you, what are you doing here in China?" Xi Wei asks, spooning crab onto my plate.

Forgetting where I am and who I am supposed to be. But I don't think I can really say that.

"Scratching around." I push the crab to one side.

"Like a pig."

"Yes."

"A pretty pig," Xi Wei laughs. Goh breaks from his conversation and catches my eyes.

I hold my hand up to the servant for more wine. In defiance of Goh's glare, I take a swig. Goh returns to his conversation.

I should reach out. I am scared. Yellow. The colour of scared. I know I won't reach out.

*

Goh and his colleagues retire to a separate room after crème brûlée is served. I assume it's to talk business. Curiously antiquated, this division of the sexes. But given that being on the game is the oldest gig going, I suppose it fits.

Jenny leads me, Lily and Rosemary to the swimming pool. The hard shine of the chemicals in the water has diminished in the dark.

We find a selection of bikinis laid out for us to wear on a spare sun lounger in the outhouse. I choose a green one.

"Mr Gu is my boyfriend. He has worked for a long time on *Meng Zhi Cheng*," Jenny says, stripped off and splashing in the water. "He is so noble, you see. He's an expert."

"What is the *Meng Zhi Cheng*?"

"It means dream city," she says. "It's for people who don't have a home. It will give them a place to start again."

I perch on the side, dabbing my feet into the cool depths before I jump in. I hold my breath and count to twenty. Surfacing again, I head for the sun loungers. I try to recline next to Lily and Rosemary but find I can't stop moving. I go back to the pool, dipping my legs in and out. The air is humid now. Too close.

Lily comes over and brushes her hand on my back.

"Why can't you relax, baby? We all just want to have a good time."

"I shouldn't be here," I say without thinking. "I'm in love with somebody. Not Goh."

She saunters over to the edge of the Jacuzzi and dips in a pedicured toe. The bubbles froth as it springs to life. Lily wades in and Rosemary joins her. "Honey," Rosemary calls, submerging herself. "Everybody here is probably in love with somebody else. But we're still having fun, aren't we?"

Wrapping myself in a towel, I walk through the patio doors. Goh's voice erupts in confrontation from my left. I make my way upstairs to the bedroom. I take the bikini off and nakedly consider my next move. Am I supposed to wait up for him, legs apart?

I lie back on the bed, trying to make a mental preparation. The ceiling has a dreamy tint with fowers carved into the cornicing. They seem to be saying, without words, 'you belong somewhere'.

My pulse drops, my eyes close. Adrift in the drowsiness of the unending thought: can you save me, please?

You, yes, you. You, yes, anyone. Anyone at all.

I think of Roman and imagine his body floating in a river.

I wait for my heart to come back and belong to me.

*

The butterfly lay down on the grass next to the woman. Her wings felt too heavy for her body. She tried and tried, but she couldn't lift them at all. The woman watched her.

"Am I dreaming you, or are you dreaming me dreaming you?" the woman said again.

Thirty

Goh isn't on the other side of the bed when I wake up in the morning. Stretching, it feels as if I'm waiting for change. For the eureka, the show down, the finale spectacle. I know it won't happen. Trousers and a linen shirt have been laid out. How funny to be so rich that you don't even need to decide what to wear in the morning. It all fits perfectly. Such a sensible outfit that I want to howl.

Downstairs, chatter comes from the same, distant room. Another meeting. So much talking. Padding away from it, I find the kitchen door propped ajar. Open plan. White, gloss, chrome and steel. Right angles and functionality. Everything is expensive and unworn. Nothing is unruffled. It really is too frigid to be a home.

Coffee brews in the stovetop kettle. The sun reflects off the black granite of the breakfast bar where a selection of teas is displayed. Chamomile. Green. Tension Tamer. Lemon Zest. What would happen if I put them all in one cup?

Wandering back through the hallway with my combination of teas, I notice that none of the handles on the many doors that line it are marked with fingerprints.

Curious about what they must all contain, I open one. There it is. A childhood daydream library. Books, books, more books. Arched ceilings. Silver wallpaper. It even has a ladder on wheels. How wonderful it would all be were it not for the context.

In the bookcase the ladder rests against, on and the third shelf up, there is a line of first editions. I run my fingers over them. Dickens, Hugo. Manna.

I pull out a copy of *Jane Eyre* in three volumes. Marbled edges and endpapers. A quarter avocado calf. I open the front cover of the first volume. The text at the bottom is smudged.

London, 1847.

I tuck the books under my arm.

It's the sort of day that you expect to be cold from indoors and provides for a shock at the warmth when you step out. Lily, Rosemary and Jenny are playing tennis dressed in garb fit for pros.

"You want to join?" Jenny yells from the furthest base line. Ball related sports not being my forté, I shake my head.

"I'll sit this one out," I call back, settling on the recliner by the patio. A servant hands me a Bloody Mary. I didn't even have to ask. This is what they call good living. I take it from him. He must be about my age.

"What's your name?" I ask.

"George." Of course.

"Thank you, George."

"Welcome, Miss."

Lily has such a strong backhand that even though she is playing on her own against Rosemary and Jenny, she's thrashing them. The crescendos of birds float up and down against the sky. One stops by the recliner and picks at a worm on the ground. It has a blue strip on its belly. Bored with the worm, it picks up a twig in its beak. Now satisfied, it flies away. I open the first book.

*

Several Bloody Marys and a skim read later, a shout comes from the tennis court, disturbing the final sentences of *Jane Eyre*. Lily is doing a lap of honour. I give her a clap as I go back into the house.

"Where is the library again?" I ask George standing silently on the patio. I'd better put the books back before anyone notices.

"The sixth door in the left hall, Miss. Would you like me to take them for you?" he says, noticing the books.

"I'll do it."

I count the doors as I walk down the left hallway. The echoes of voices in debate are softer now; it's not clear where they are coming from. Sixth door on the right or the left? I opt for the right.

Opening, I realise I'm wrong: it's a bar complete with dancefloor. Under the disco ball is a pool table. The room is clouded with smoke. The voices rise in volume from beside the window, where I make out Goh leaning over the low table surrounded by his associates. His face beams red as he drags from a cigar. Stubbing the butt in the ashtray, he picks up a blueprint at the top of a pile of paper. He repeats the same words in Chinese over and over. Each time, the way he says the phrase increases in volume and agitation.

Intuition calls hard. I shouldn't be here. Of course, my feet tell me to walk away. But they won't.

Gu gets up and makes for the door. Goh yells after him; it's a verbal assault. Gu says something back without turning around, then he notices me.

"Well!" Gu says, with mock cheer. "You caught us!"

The business partners glance at each other.

"What are you doing here?" Goh asks.

I hold up the volumes of *Jane Eyre*.

"Where's the library?" My question comes out all jittery.

"Ask the *ayi*!" Goh's tone strains in an attempt at mildness.

The voices continue to joust accusingly long after I have closed the door. Ugly talking.

*

The hot water runs into the ceramic of the bath. The steam clings to the mirror, slowly clouding over any human resemblance reflected. Mystify. Demystify.

I lever myself in, turning bright pink as I sit down. It feels good to boil. Like I deserve it. I dunk my head into the water. Presence. Dispersion. Diffusion. Water into air. Air into nothing. I could lie under here for hours. I could never resurface.

A knock from afar. I scramble out of the bath and don the robe, reaching the bedroom as Wu Yi bursts in and rushes to the window. Agitated, she points to a black Mercedes, its lights disappearing as it speeds down the drive.

"What happened?"

"There is no dinner," Wu Yi says. "They all left, it's over."

Perhaps this is it.

"But don't you go!" she calls as I run out.

Downstairs, the door into the bar is open. There's nobody there now, save Goh who is lying on the sofa with his eyes closed. A half consumed bottle of gin is open next him. I perch on the edge of the sofa and brush his foot with my hand. For a second he struggles to recognise me.

"If I ever see those fuckers again..." he starts. "It's all ruined. They're selfish cunts. It's all ego. We spent years on this, but all they care about is the prestige. The politics. The money's not talking enough."

Knowing a bit about disappointment by now, I have the impulse to be intimate. I put my arm on his back. He shrugs it off and hands me a gin. Holds his out. I hold mine out. We take a sip, staring at each other. This energy is too much. I stand up.

"Where are you going?" he shouts. This again.

"Nowhere."

"Fuck this!" Goh says, "I need to hit something."

His anguish fills the room. I take a step back.

"Oh, for god's sake! I'm not going to hit you! What do you expect?"

"I have no expectations, or I wouldn't be here."

I sink the rest of the gin and bang the glass on the table. I go to the door. I open it and I put my body through. I close it behind me and walk up the stairs to the bedroom. Fuck this, fuck the money and fuck Goh. Where can I go? How can I leave? How can I get there?

Goh catches me up in the bedroom.

"Sorry," he says, putting his hand on my arm.

I watch as he goes to the armoire by the dresser. Inside, a mini bar and a record player. He chooses from a rack of about twenty seven inches. A blues song I don't recognise floats from speakers as he lights a spliff. We both take a draw. The room is instantly more forgiving.

We lie next to each other on the bed. His face seems softer now. I'm with the room. It is right and it is whole and pure again.

"Why are you doing this?" he says. "You obviously hate it. And you aren't very good at pretending not to."

"I'm writing a book. I can't stick at a job. And I need to leave Shanghai."

"What's your book about?" he takes another drag.

"A butterfly." I'm naked now, whether I'm wearing clothes or not. He puts a hand up to my cheek. Gentle, this feeling. Not shameful.

"I like you," he says. "I like that you're terrible at pretending. But you're quite bright."

"I'm not smart. I wouldn't be doing this if I were."

His hand drops from my face. As he stands up I can feel its imprint on my skin. The spliff lies in the ashtray. Another toke. I am in until the end.

"I'll read it when you're finished, give you an honest opinion." No suggestion of sarcasm.

Touched more than I can tell him, I stand up and wrap my hands around his waist from behind. His muscles tighten as if he is afraid. Maybe we both should be. His dream room has driven off in a Mercedes. Mine is written in notebooks underneath the mattress of a bed in a hostel.

A crumpled man-giant now, Goh reaches round to rest his hand on my cheek again. I kiss the back of his neck. He turns. His lips hit my forehead. My eyelids. I wonder if we can't make each other better.

We move over to the bed. Between the extremes of hot and cold; between symmetry and asymmetry, breadth and width. This is colour. Filling gaps between spaces, between black and white. The robe comes off. It falls to the floor, a puddle of provocation. Desire gives the hunger. Hunger gives the need. Need gives the action. It is painful not to have it. I want it. I want him.

*

The butterfly felt a stir of agitation. How should she know who was dreaming who? In the end, this was just another transformation of things.

"I am losing the ability to wonder," the butterfly thought, without regret.

Thirty-one

Trying to forget things you don't want to remember is the best motivational tool there is. I place the final full-stop on what was originally the final page but now occurs in the middle and lean back in the chair of the all-night café I have been frequenting for the past two weeks.

Today is Wednesday, I believe. It's six or seven am judging by the radiance of the sky. I have finished a pile of paper that I might consider calling a book. It's not good enough. It's never going to be good enough. But it's done. Is this an achievement? Unfamiliar with achievement, I consider the question. Yes, yes this probably could be considered an achievement. Even for those with insufferably low self-esteem. A new mother, I feel joy and fear at the same time. But at least I birthed the thing.

This. Is. It.

Entirely necessary: a celebration of the finest order.

I go out onto the main road where there the occasional pedestrian attempts the newness of the day. I walk in no particular direction, paying scant attention to the signs, the catcalls, the ebb and flow of the bodies on the pavement. The shriek of shutters being opened is accompanied by the burr of shifting cars. The streets are alien again.

I suspend my notions of time and space. Instead, I soak up the sense of freedom that comes from being released from a chain that has long exerted a stranglehold, real or imagined.

*

Jia Ma is putting the chalkboards outside as I reach *Gilded Balloon*. She gives a jokey salute. I dance across the road and wordlessly wrap her in as big a hug as I can muster on fifty-three hours of working.

The writing hangover is kicking in but elation pushes it back down.

"You're happy," she says, puzzled. I stop hugging her.

"I finished the book!" I yell, "Yes, I am happy! I am happy!"

Inside, Jia Ma pours fresh coffee. We clink mugs.

"You look... how you say... rough as guts."

"I don't give a toss."

"We have to celebrate," she says. "I'll get Susie to cover the evening shift. Whatever you want."

Whatever I want. That would be a fine suggestion if I knew what this was. A bedraggled man, the first patron of the day, comes in. Jia Ma whips out of her seat. The man orders blueberry pancakes. Jia Ma goes off into the kitchen.

Just as I have an idea, my remaining energy evaporates. I doze off, perched on the stool.

*

"Fore!" Rose shouts as she swings the rusty club and cracks at the ball, which arcs up and over, narrowly avoiding a stray attendant beside the sign marked with the number one hundred. The attendant crouches down and holds his hands over his head. His basket of balls drops onto the Astroturf and they roll off into the crevices from which he has just extricated them.

"She shoots, she scores!" I yell.

I finish the rest of my beer and step up to the tee. I gave up golf when I was nineteen after the incident involving a five iron on my seventh date with the Brazilian named Jesus. It hurt to lose Jesus.

I try not to think about the time spent in A&E and his damaged eyesight as I look towards the signs. The fifty-metre mark may be a reasonable expectation. I line my fingers up and take aim. I mishit. The ball swerves to the left, landing in a pool of rainwater.

"Bugger." I reach for my beer. Jia Ma tees up.

"Go on!" Rose hollers. "Show that ball who's boss!"

Jia Ma pads her feet. Her shot similarly vanishes into a never land

177

on the right-hand side of the green. Rose does a victory dance.

"How did you get to be so good?" I ask Rose as we pack up.

"An ex-boyfriend was semi-pro," she sniffs.

"Your ex-boyfriends seem to have taught you a lot," Jia Ma tells Rose, with such sincerity that I find it difficult not to laugh.

*

As she closed her eyes for what would be the last time, the butterfly wasn't sad. She wasn't sad when she found she couldn't feel her wings at all. She wasn't sad that she would never see the grass, or the trees, or Red Admiral again. She wasn't sad about any of that because she had lost the ability to wonder.

Thirty-two

The cherry blossoms in the lobby of the *Peace Hotel*, pink as a child's cheek on a spring day, soften a space otherwise peppered with austere gold columns. It was a novelty to ask for the best room in the house. But despite having means, I remain resolutely anti-materialistic. Apart from the one new dress I am wearing, purchased yesterday. And the new shoes that go with the dress. And the leather-bound notebook.

Arriving intentionally late, I make my way to the designated spot in the already crowded downstairs bar. Jazz flows from the on-stage trio. She isn't there yet. A surge of relief creeps into my gut. Why do this? Masochism? Maybe. Clarity? Partly.

I order a vodka from the glossy bar girl. Looking around, I wonder what category the surrounding expatriates fit into. From the quality of the suits, my guess is that most of them are new-colonialists who are probably benefiting rather well from the leniencies in contractual law. Perhaps this is what it looks like to make a killing.

"Ruby," comes a voice from behind me.

Memory turns those left on bad terms into caricatures. Amanda had become stockier, her face more shadowed. Standing in front of me, she's a lovely a young woman again, her camera swinging from her neck. In the sheen of the evening, she gives off a dusky glow.

We take a seat by the stage where the trio wind down for the night.

"I was surprised when you called," she says. "What do you want?"

"I wanted you to tell me about it. About you and him. I want to understand."

She stirs her drink, unable to meet my eyes. The trio start to pack up for the night behind her.

"It was always like that," she says, "The way it was with you. Since I met him. We have this thing for years. It comes and goes. Often, we would have other people involved, too. Whether or not it's love, I don't know. I met him when I was thirteen and he was eighteen. He was the first man for me. He broke me in. It never went away. I think he loved you, though."

"It's not that simple." I don't doubt it, but I don't want to talk about it with her. "He called me. After he left. I told the police."

"What did he say?"

"I wouldn't talk to him."

"After you left, he couldn't take it. I thought he was depressed. I've seen him like that before over girls. That morning, he left without saying goodbye. By the evening I hadn't heard from him so I check with his family. They don't know where he is. I have to tell them everything. About us, about you and him." She leans back in her chair. "He did the same thing as you."

"I guess neither of us is very good at dealing with reality."

We watch as the trio pull their instruments off the stage, their cases bumping fuzzily on the carpet.

"I wonder where he is."

"I wonder, too."

The tension dissipates with the crowd. Is this a conclusion?

"I need to go," she says.

When we reach her padlocked bicycle parked on Nanjing Road, Amanda hugs me for longer than seems comfortable for either of us. Pulling away, she takes a snap of me standing there before I can say no. Perhaps I should tell her that I am leaving. I can't do it.

"I miss him," she says, mounting the bike.

"I know."

I watch her peddle off. Up full to the light the legs placed on the pavement walk. And it's not the space between that dictates. Rather, the other side of the road. Listen to the tap of your feet as they hit the pavement. The tap, tap, tap. Then, hit the road, Jack.

I take a long route back to the *Peace Hotel*, avoiding shouts and catcalls. All cities, every day, are privy to deaths. Who turns that endless wheel? Who keeps the dead from the living? This is where I stop, start, get through. The city is an insomniac. It doesn't stop to listen to you. But it will, if you hang on, eventually make you smile.

*

Waiting in the reception area of Goh's company headquarters, I realise it could double as a landing area for characters in any of the *Alien Predator* series. A silver desk is surrounded by staff manning switchboards. I pick up an expatriate magazine, *About Town*. Rose is in a few of the pictures from some restaurant opening or other. Goh's assistant tells me to go in. I dust myself off. It's like entering an examination. One that might matter.

Several other members of staff share Goh's room with him although he is separated off by glass dividers. He ushers me inside, pulling the screens down. The twenty notebooks are piled neatly in front of him.

"Did you receive the money?"

"Yes," I reply. "Thank you."

"Okay," he says, pointing to the Moleskines. "I don't have a lot of time. You are not a genius."

Immediate deflation.

"But you're good for your age. Is this the only copy you have?"

"That's it, all in notebooks."

"Do you not want to type it out? There's a computer..." He points behind me. I turn around. My nemesis. A thirty-inch Mac.

"No," I reply.

"Tell you what. If you type it out I can probably think of a publisher who will read it for you. A friend."

"You *know* people? In a networking kind of a way?"

"Yes, I know people in a networking kind of a way," he laughs.

Of course he knows people.

"Don't think so much," he adds. "Just do."

*

After I have said my goodbyes to Jia Ma and the *Gilded Balloon*, I meet Rose in the centre of People's Park at sunset. We settle on one of the benches outside the metro stop with an ice cream each. Kites mill in the sky. Both are being led by kids. The yellow one overtakes the red. The colours flit back and forth in airy competition.

"Forget what you did," Rose says, her voice decisive. "You're leaving anyway. Make yourself a new person again."

Forgetting everything: making things new.

"What are you going to do?" I ask.

"Stick around here, I guess. See how things work out. I'm not going back to Australia. I don't know what I would do there, now. How I would live. I'm getting used to this place. I think I can make a go of it."

We make the trek to our old flat, through the winding streets. When we get there, a computer-generated image of a new high-rise hangs on the front of the wire fence. The design is another boxy affair. This is progress.

Rose gives me a leg up over the wire fence. As I jump down and walk in, she hangs back, peering through the wire.

Only the inside of the downstairs neighbours' basement flat is still there, although no more than a shell. An old pair of shoes lies on the floor in what was their kitchen, the soles upturned as though waving a white flag. A topless workman cooks noodles over a stove. Pantaloons hang from bamboo poles.

"Don't you think that if China were involved in a freak nuclear attack, and one thing were to remain, it would be bamboo poles with big underwear?" Rose asks.

"Probably."

Hearing us, the workman gets up and starts to yell angrily in Shanghainese. I retreat back over the fence.

"Where do you think they went?" I ask Rose, as she helps me down. The workman mutters but goes back to his noodles.

"They might have been re-homed."

All that being said and all bets being off, we float on until we reach the metro.

We embrace for a long time without saying anything.

"Enjoy yourself," I tell her.

"You, too. Wherever the hell you end up. Come back if you can't take a normal life."

We say we will keep in touch, that she will come and visit me. All those things you express with true intentions. I turn away.

"This, it's all temporary," Rose says, serious again.

There it is. That grandness I love and pity at the same time. The myriad of oscillations. With her watching my back, I make my way through the entrance. I turn around. She waves.

"I'll miss you," I call. I don't know if she hears me.

I reach the lift and press the button. As the doors shut behind me and the metal cell jerks to the lower level, I realise I will never see Rose again.

*

As the butterfly faded, she thought, "I wasn't here for happiness. I just existed to be beautiful, to give other people pleasure."

Beauty was very useful but in the end it didn't stop the elements, or the world from turning. Neither did happiness and sorrow.

As the butterfly stopped living, it was only a brief bloom that withered. It was only the flight of those wings that left a mark.

Thirty-three

Airports are never the ending of choice for great heroines. The queue has reached the traditional standoff beside the departure gate. Hungover gap-year students with long hair are resting on oversized backpacks with their heads buried in individual copies of *The Cheapskates' Guide To Asia*. I step over them.

I pass the ticket to the pristine airhostess who welcomes me onto the craft. "Have a great day," she says.

"I'm sure I will," I reply.

On board, I'm waved to First Class. "Would you like the pink champagne or the regular champagne, Miss?" another mahogany tanned hostess asks, handing me a newspaper. Decisions, decisions.

"Pink, please."

I scan the newspaper. There is a four-page exposé about a terrorist attack on a transatlantic flight. Images of mangled metal. Big and useless words. The guy on the other side of the aisle takes a copy from the hostess, reads the cover and starts to wheeze in fear.

"Don't panic, baby, I'm here for you," his girlfriend says, pulling him close. The guy's panic attack subsides.

Fear of crashing is as crippling as fear of failure. When you look at the plane – there now, outside – you can see how still it is. You know that when you get on you will go up, and for a while you won't be able to see anything. You'll make it over countries that you haven't been to yet, all in the comfort of your own separate seat with the radio on.

Roads will lie untravelled, and you'll be listening with the radio on. An ocean will fly beneath you, and you'll still be listening with the radio on. Ice will melt and the oceans will become a bit deeper, and you'll still be listening with the radio on. The whole world will turn below you, and you'll still be listening with the radio on.

If you're lucky, you will come to know how insignificant you are. Your life does not matter. You can always make it new again.

At least we're together, these hundred strangers and me. For these ten hours, we can live as one. If I do have children I'll tell them to talk to strangers. Being a stranger, you have to remind yourself of who you are when you meet someone new. Each time you let go, you are left to wonder whether you the sort of person who is forgettable. Are you?

The pilot's voice comes over the intercom. Burblings about weather, safety, time. You have to allow those moments before take-off, when you wonder what would happen if the plane were to crash. If you were to go down in a ball of flames. What would your last thoughts be? I would think about the people I have seen and not talked to. For me, it's like reading a book.

I put my headphones on. Beethoven's *Ninth Symphony* streams out. The plane moves forward. Lights hit the tarmac outside, illuminating a slogan on the concrete below. *Bright Future City.* The dragon opens its mouth. The vignettes of city life – which, when colliding, give it its essence – are already becoming memories.

I close my eyes and think of my new suitcases full of notebooks and dresses. Every second somewhere in the world a hundred planes take off. This one takes me.

Goodbye, Shanghai. It is – it was – a pleasure.

*

The woman woke up. Noticing the dead body of the butterfly, she picked it up and slipped it into the pocket of her summer dress. With that, she started the trek back to the city. Back to the lights.

Acknowledgements

The author wishes to acknowledge Xiaowen Zhu, Dan W. Jones, Heather Morgan, Maureen Freely, Sally Thomson and Kenneth Brydon.